Under Siege!

Robyn Gioia

Pineapple Press, Inc.
Sarasota, Florida

Inquiries should be addressed to:
Pineapple Press, Inc.
P.O. Box 3889
Sarasota, Florida 34230
www.pineapplepress.com

Library of Congress Cataloging in Publication Data

Names: Gioia, Robyn, author.
Title: Under siege! / by Robyn Gioia.
Description: Sarasota, Florida : Pineapple Press, 2016. | Summary: "At 13, Pedro and Miguel are too young to fight, but they realize they must sneak behind enemy lines to help, or the town of St. Augustine may perish during the siege of 1702"-- Provided by publisher.
Identifiers: LCCN 2016010184 (print) | LCCN 2016024451 (ebook) | ISBN 9781561649648 (pbk.) | ISBN 9781561649662 ()
Subjects: | CYAC: Sieges--Fiction. | Saint Augustine (Fla.)--History--Siege, 1702--Fiction. | Florida--History--Spanish colony, 1565-1763--Fiction.
Classification: LCC PZ7.1.G58 Un 2016 (print) | LCC PZ7.1.G58 (ebook) | DDC
  [Fic]--dc23
LC record available at https://lccn.loc.gov/2016010184

First Edition
10 9 8 7 6 5 4 3 2 1

Design by Carol Lynne Knight

Printed and bound in the USA

*To the people of every nation
who have helped shape the history
of the United States of America*

Contents

Map of St. Augustine and the Events of the Siege in 1702   *vi–vii*

UNDER SIEGE!   1

Author's Note   *183*

Historical Notes   *184*

Glossary   *186*

Acknowledgments   *191*

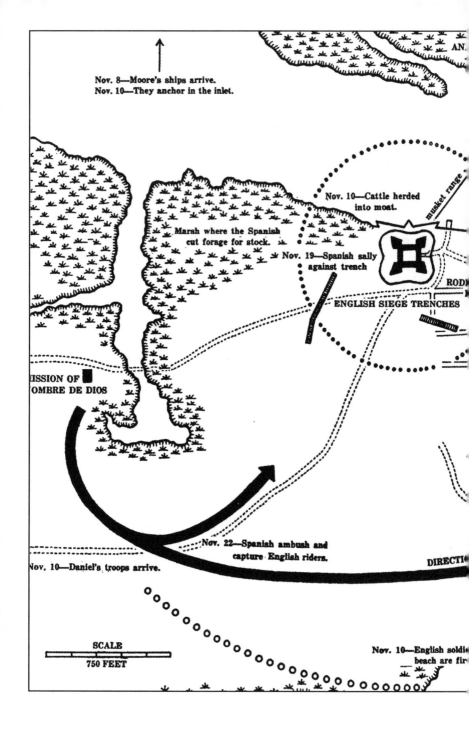

Nov. 8—Moore's ships arrive.
Nov. 10—They anchor in the inlet.

AN.

Nov. 10—Cattle herded into moat.

Marsh where the Spanish cut forage for stock.

Nov. 19—Spanish sally against trench

musket range

RODE

ENGLISH SIEGE TRENCHES

IISSION OF
OMBRE DE DIOS

Nov. 22—Spanish ambush and capture English riders.

DIRECTI

Nov. 10—Daniel's troops arrive.

SCALE
750 FEET

Nov. 10—English soldie
beach are fir

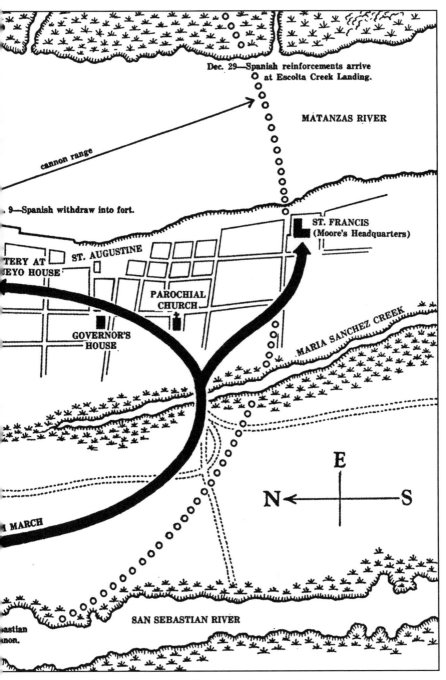

Dec. 29—Spanish reinforcements arrive at Escolta Creek Landing.

MATANZAS RIVER

cannon range

9—Spanish withdraw into fort.

ST. FRANCIS (Moore's Headquarters)

TERY AT EYO HOUSE

ST. AUGUSTINE

PAROCHIAL CHURCH

GOVERNOR'S HOUSE

MARIA SANCHEZ CREEK

E

N ← → S

MARCH

astian nou.

SAN SEBASTIAN RIVER

This diagram was prepared by Historians Luis R Arana and Albert Manucy of the National Park Service staff at Castillo de San Marcos, from the Spanish descriptions of the siege. The topography is from the Arredondo "Plan de la Ciudad de San Agustín" of 1737 (AI 87-1-2 /2)

Much of this historical adventure was inspired by the 1702 attack on America's Ancient City, St. Augustine, Florida.

1

New World

THE MAN FELT HIS STRENGTH slipping away. He stumbled awkwardly down the riverbank. Every muscle in his body ached. His head throbbed and his senses had dulled. He could barely stay awake. He felt like he was going to fall facedown and not get up. The only thing driving him forward was his fear of being caught.

Looking back over his shoulder, he strained to see if anyone followed in the woods. A rustling noise erupted in a patch of underbrush. Shifting uneasily to the ground, he rolled awkwardly under a patch of palmettos. Mosquitoes buzzed along his ears, nose, and every exposed area of his body but he dared not move. Long, sharp palmetto blades bit against his skin but he turned his mind away from his wretched shelter, spit the sandy grit from his mouth, and pressed his lips together, daring not to breathe. Noise would carry to enemy ears. Had the heathen Indians tracked him across the river? Unable to take another step, he curled up in a ball.

✳✳✳

"PEDRO, HURRY! The gopher tortoise is getting away!" shouted Miguel.

Not knowing what to expect, Miguel stabbed the end of his sawed-off quarter-pike next to the gnarly trunk of an oak tree and ran toward a wide hole in the ground. He bent down and peered inside the opening beneath the thicket. A black interior met his eyes.

I laughed at the sight of my friend's head inside a tortoise burrow. "You can forget about eating tortoise soup today. That burrow goes back thirty foot lengths and I don't think your arms are that long."

Chuckling to myself, I wiped the perspiration from my face and the back of my neck. The heat was typical for this time of year, hot and humid enough to keep you miserable all day long. After stopping to adjust the position of my father's old but treasured bow, I tucked my axe, one that had cost me two alligator skins, back into my belt. A familiar chorus of noisy tree frogs croaked in the background as the rain splashed across the canopy of trees.

"Come, Miguel," I said. "I want to look for some river cane before heading back to town. My supply of arrows is getting low."

I passed the quarter-pike back to my friend and we headed deeper into the woods. Trees stretched as far as the eye could see. I watched Miguel climbing awkwardly over the ground cover, realizing how fortunate I was to have him as a friend. As newcomers from Spain, Miguel's family had joined their relatives in service at the Castillo de San Marcos in St. Augustine.

Most of the townspeople were *criollos,* locals of Spanish descent who had been born and raised in the New World. My grandpapa proudly told the story of how Admiral Pedro Menéndez de Avilés founded the town of St. Augustine 137 years earlier in 1565. The Admiral had been searching for a place to start a military post along the La Florida coastline. He named it St. Augustine in honor of St. Augustine of Hippo. Privateers, pirates, and thieves lay in wait for Her Majesty's ships carrying goods and precious metals back to Spain. From this location, Spain would be able to protect her territories and the treasure fleet sailing along the Gulf Stream. It was the Admiral's name of Pedro that I carried: Pedro Manuel Fernández Moreno.

I pointed Miguel, formally known as Miguel Antonio Ortiz, toward the heart of the woods, where even denser ground cover filled the terrain. We stepped onto a dry area where cypress knees normally stood above the low-lying water. Next to the swamp lay a thick path of dry pine needles and pinecones shed by a forest of towering pine trees. A layer of crunchy palm fronds also crackled underfoot.

"I will look for an opossum," Miguel said hopefully. "They are so slow I could catch one with my sack."

I nudged him, trying not to display my amusement. "They

sleep during the day and an opossum tastes foul. Its meat tires the jaws."

Miguel frowned.

I had to concentrate on keeping a straight face. "But rattle-snake meat is tender and it satisfies the stomach. Its bite can kill a horse and the man riding it, too. Keep your eyes open and be careful where you step. They nest all along here."

Miguel looked warily at the ground before glancing up at me.

I swallowed my chuckle. Something inside me found pleasure in taking advantage of Miguel's naiveté. He had arrived from Toledo, Spain, a modern city full of marketplaces and theaters. I could tell by the look on his face that Miguel had never walked in the deep woods before, let alone encountered a snake that might grow to be eight foot lengths.

Miguel searched our surroundings, his anxious face combing the area. "We will look for rattlers if you say so, Pedro."

I stifled another laugh. The uncertainty in Miguel's voice was perfect. Then a feeling or remorse came over me. Thinking it cruel to worry my friend any further, I decided to relieve him of his anxiety.

"We'll hunt no rattlers today. We can stop at the rocks next to the Castillo and chip oysters off to take home. They have shells that can slice the hide off a buffalo, if we had some here in La Florida, so be careful not to slip."

Miguel's pinched expression relaxed. I laughed so hard, my sides began to ache. He was good natured, something he would need to survive in La Florida's harsh surroundings.

In the distance, a flock of wood storks searched a pool of standing water for insects. A wild calico pig darted across the ground in front of us. Speed helped it slip safely into the thicket before Miguel could catch it.

As usual, the mosquitoes hovered in swarms waiting for any warm-blooded animal to come near. I swatted unsuccessfully at the bloodsuckers before stopping to remove Grandmamma's insect repellent from my pouch. Made from wax myrtle, it helped fend off the biting beasts. After generously slathering the ointment across my skin and hair, I offered it to Miguel, who did not refuse.

Fortunately, my grandmamma had placed her specially made

insect repellent inside my pouch this very morning. If anyone knew how to survive in such harsh surroundings, it was she, the town's wise woman. My Spanish grandpapa had taken a local Timucua Indian woman for a wife. Women were scarce in a military town of men. Many of the native Timucua married into and became part of the Spanish culture. It was my Timucua Grandmamma Leena who taught me the ways of the land. That also made me a *mestizo*, a descendant of both the Timucua and Spanish cultures.

We continued our journey until we reached the banks of the St. Johns River. The pungent scent of river water hung in the air but it was the faint sounds of a human voice that caught my attention. Blocking Miguel with my arm, I raised a finger to my lips.

"Someone is close," I whispered.

We moved in, being careful not to make any sounds ourselves.

"And he's praying," Miguel added quietly.

I pulled him into a squatting position. "English scouts have been spotted traveling from the north in search of free blacks and Indians loyal to Spain," I said in a soft whisper. "They catch them and sell them as slaves. It might be a captive or a runaway."

Miguel's forehead wrinkled. "Or perhaps it is a scout. Would it not be wise to make our way back into town?"

Running away was not in my blood and I bristled at the idea. I couldn't help snorting. "I am only one year under the special fighting age of fourteen and you, Miguel, are the same. We are almost men. Do you not want to know why a strange man is in the woods praying so far away from the settlements? No one knows this territory better than me. Scouts wouldn't know where to find us if we ran."

Throwing caution to the wind, I stepped boldly into the opening and looked around.

"Who's there?" asked a soft, raspy voice.

A thin man kneeling at the edge of the riverbank spotted me. A patch of trampled palmetto leaves revealed a hiding place behind him. His sunken cheeks hung under eyes ringed with dark circles. A ripped tunic hung limply from his body.

Miguel stepped out beside me. The man wore Spanish clothes but carried no supplies or weapons and a horse was nowhere in sight. Bloody scratches covered his arms and face. I searched the riverbank, expecting to see a canoe. There was none.

"Who are you and why are you here?" I asked.

The man struggled to stand. Exhaustion lowered him back to the ground. His scratchy voice cracked when he spoke. "I have come to speak with Governor Zúñiga in St. Augustine. Pray tell, how far is my travel?"

Seeing the terrible thirst in the man's eyes, I took my canteen from my side, opened the spout, and offered him some water. Shaky hands lifted the container from my grasp. He drank in gulps.

"My friend and I are from St. Augustine. It is one league as the crow flies east."

It was the man's turn to study us. "You are from the stone Castillo? The fort, Castillo de San Marcos?"

We nodded.

The man bowed his head in silence; words too softly to hear passed from his lips. When he looked up again the creased lines in his face had softened.

"Then the Lord has answered my prayers. Native Indians loyal to England have been pursuing me for three days. My horse was injured, I have lost my weapons and supplies, and I have been running on foot through woods and swamp for many, many leagues. I have an urgent message for the governor. My talk with him is urgent. The lives of your people depend on it."

2

Governor Zúñiga

Attack him where he is unprepared, appear where you are not expected. — Sun Tzu

MIGUEL AND I STRUGGLED to support the man as we climbed slowly through the thick patches of palmetto in the mosquito-infested swamp. Now that there were three of us, thoughts of running out of wax myrtle insect repellent crossed my mind. We stopped only briefly to rest. My neck and shoulders ached from holding the man's weight. Crossing through low-lying water offered us some protection against trackers but lengthened our journey. Indians loyal to England would understand the ways of the land and that meant we had to push ahead no matter how slowly.

Miguel gripped the man from the other side. He clenched his teeth under the strain of the man's weight, but continued on in silence. The sun had set by the time we reached the neighborhoods surrounding the Castillo.

The fort, the Castillo de San Marcos, had been built between 1672 and 1695. Coquina, an indigenous stone made from the small shells of the coquina clam, had been quarried from nearby Anastasia Island to make its sturdy walls. A diamond-shaped bastion guarded each corner of the square structure, making it look like a castle. An open courtyard lay in the middle.

On finally reaching the Castillo door, I pounded urgently. "It's Pedro Manuel! Call my uncle. I have a messenger from San Luis and he has important information for the governor. Let us in!"

My pimply-faced cousin opened the door. The *pantalones* of Nico's uniform lay in heaps across his shoes and the sleeves fell well past his hands. He looked at Miguel, then at me. I expected the next thing to happen and he did not disappoint.

A sneer crept from one ear to the other. "Who do we have here? It seems my little cousin knocks. Have you come to see the life of real men?"

"Not now, Nico," I sighed. "I have not come to trade insults with you. I am in need of the *capitán*, right now."

Nico smirked. "I hold the title of soldier and you do not. Poor fatherless Pedro has to sit at home and make dolls for the *niños* out of cornhusks, so his mama can sell them in her store. There is no man to teach him. He learns from two women and a babbling cripple."

I seethed. "Just let me in. We can see about all that later."

Nico glared at me. I pushed him aside and lunged through the door. Miguel and the messenger stumbled through behind me.

"Hand him over to me," snapped a clearly vexed Nico. "I will deliver him to the proper authorities. You must run home now like a good little *niño*."

"He is mine to deliver," I answered, straightening my back to its full height so I loomed over him.

Nico's nostrils flared. "Hand him to me, or he will not go at all."

The hairs on the back of my neck began to bristle. Fortunately, I did not have to act.

An officer walked into the room. "What is all this commotion? Is that you I hear, young Pedro? What could possibly be so urgent?" Then he caught sight of the man in our arms, and ordered Nico to empty a chair. "Whom do we have here?"

Miguel helped lower our guest into the seat.

"He has brought an important message for the governor. We found him near where the otters play along the St. Johns," I said.

The officer flagged Nico to his side. "Nico, tell the sergeant to find Governor Zúñiga and tell him he is urgently needed."

Before leaving the room, Nico turned and glared at me. I raised my hand just high enough so the others could not see and waved good-bye. He left the room, his tight face glowering in response. I am not ashamed to admit I took pleasure in that little torment.

As much as I hated letting Nico under my skin, he triumphed in making my blood boil. Yes, my father had died when I was a baby, but he died an honorable death fighting for the crown. At least I assumed he died an honorable death. When I ask, no one will speak of it. Could my father have possibly dishonored the town in some way?

To vex me further, Nico is not alone in his unjust treatment of me. A portion of the townspeople pity me because I am growing up without a father. They fault my mother for not remarrying. Well, I don't want or need their pity. To pity someone is to expect less of them. They do not see me for who I am. This is the cross I must bear until I am old enough to take my place among the soldiers.

The sergeant hurried through the door only moments after Nico's departure. The light from his lantern grew smaller as he disappeared down the road.

"Pedro, offer our guest some food while I summon the men," commanded the officer.

I poured the weary messenger a goblet of wine before handing him a small loaf of bread and a small chunk of cheese. The man crossed himself in prayer before drinking greedily and tearing a large chunk of bread from the crust. His repast did not last long as he consumed the contents of his plate in gulps. I realized the man had suffered greatly in his efforts to get to the Castillo. What could be so important that he risked so much, I wondered?

A royal officer entered the room.

"Uncle Manuel!" I ran to his side.

Formally known as Juan Manuel Fernández Moreno, the man I called uncle held my shoulders back and looked directly into my eyes. "The governor is on his way. Now tell me what has happened, Pedro. Tell me all, nephew."

The story poured from my lips of how we came to find the messenger, our fear of being tracked by natives loyal to England, and our slow difficult journey back to St. Augustine. My uncle paced back and forth in front of the fireplace, his head bowed as he listened.

When I finished, he waved at the door. "Pedro, it is time to return home. This is the governor's business now."

"But Uncle, Miguel and I have carried this man for many leagues. We want to know what he has to say."

Just then Governor Joseph de Zúñiga y Zerda entered the room flanked by soldiers. I couldn't help but look admiringly at the commanding figure, the *gobernador y capitán general*. As supreme commander and *Capitán General* of La Florida, the governor had a reputation for being a wise leader. I dreamed of being just like him one day.

Many soldiers entered the room. The commotion afforded us the break Miguel and I needed. Pushing Miguel behind the open door, I whispered, "Shhh . . . if we stay out of the way, my uncle might not send us away. They have taken little notice of us."

We listened as Uncle Manuel reported the details of how we came upon the stranger at the riverbank.

Zúñiga turned toward the stranger and placed a hand on his shoulder. "You have done well to reach your destination. The Crown acknowledges your loyalty and devotion to the Spanish territories. Now, pray tell me of this urgent news."

The messenger tried to stand, but his weariness forced him back in his seat. A shaky hand pulled a letter slowly from the inside of his tattered tunic and pressed it into the governor's outstretched hand. His voice cracked as he struggled to clear his throat.

"I have been sent by Capitán Juan Solana and Capitán Francisco Romo de Uriza of . . . of . . . of San Luis to deliver this message. Six days ago, a Christian Chacato woman, who had traveled weeks with her infant, came to the mission bearing news of an English attack. The English governor of Ca . . . Carolina, Governor Moore, intends to lead one hundred small boats down the Atlantic coast in an attack on St. Augustine."

Alarm broke out amongst the soldiers. Shock gripped my insides. I instinctively placed a hand over Miguel's mouth to keep him quiet while biting my own lip to keep silent.

A deep crease formed across the governor's brow, but he did not speak. All eyes shifted to Zúñiga, waiting for his response. He bent down on his knees and gently lifted the messenger's chin to study his eyes.

The fear inside me grew. I knew the Castillo did not have enough men, weapons, or provisions to stop an attack. Even worse, the Castillo wouldn't be able to hold out for reinforcements. It would take weeks, if not months, to get help from Havana and it would be an even longer journey to get help from Spain.

Panic filled me with dread as the impact of the messenger's words hit me. I had only known safety at the Castillo. My family and friends were in danger. All of our lives were in danger. This was not a skirmish far in the distance. This threatened the very ground we stood upon. I reached for the axe handle tucked inside my belt.

Miguel's shaky voice spoke next to me. "What are we to do, Pedro?"

I grabbed Miguel's trembling hands. Trying to steady my own at the same time, I concentrated on the sound of my voice. "I do not know, my friend. We must pray the governor is wise in his decisions."

Governor Zúñiga cleared his throat. I shifted to get a better look at his face from behind the door's edge. The crease had disappeared from the governor's forehead and equanimity now covered his face. Standing with his back straight and his voice certain, the governor gave his command. "Men, sound the alarm. It is urgent I speak with all the townspeople."

3

The English

To secure ourselves against defeat lies in our own hands,
but the opportunity of defeating the enemy
is provided by the enemy himself. — Sun Tzu

UPON RETURNING HOME, I quickly kneeled before a small statue of the Madonna in the comfort of my home and whispered a prayer. St. Augustine would need Her help if we were to withstand an attack from such a powerful enemy. The bell on the lookout tower rang, its heavy clang sounding the alarm for all to hear. Within seconds, the church bells followed. Neighborhood windows dark with night began to glow with candlelight.

"Pedro, help your grandpapa to the Castillo. The church bells have sharpened his mind. We will go to the Castillo as a family," said my mother, Maria, from the doorway. On her shoulder leaned my elderly grandpapa, Diego.

Grandmamma Leena hugged Grandpapa from the other side. Racing to stand beside her, I lifted my grandmamma's arm out from around Grandpapa's side where she held him in place. I straightened my back and pulled Grandpapa up by the belt, trying to match her height. Before relinquishing her grip, Grandmamma Leena ran her hand lovingly across his brow and patted me affectionately on the cheek. Then she fell in behind us.

"Are you in pain, Grandpapa? Should I stand a little higher?" I whispered.

"Do not worry about me, grandson. Hurry, Pedro. We have been summoned."

I remembered when my Grandpapa answered the call of duty proudly and earned the respect of every soldier. Advancing age and many long years of service to the crown have taken their toll. Some days his mind is sharp, during others he slumps into childishness.

Despite his frailties, to my eyes, he is still that commanding soldier from long ago.

"Grandson, do you know why the bells ring?" he asked.

"The English are coming from Carolina to attack the Castillo and capture St. Augustine."

He paused, but kept his thoughts to himself. A private man, he considered all things carefully. "Is that so? Do not worry about your grandpapa's aches and pains. If the governor calls, then the importance is great."

My mother looked sternly toward the south. "If your brothers had not moved to Mexico, they would help defend the Castillo."

"I will fight, Mama," I said. "I can shoot a trabuco, Grandpapa knows I'm an expert with a bow, and I can wield a machete and axe as well as my brothers, if not better. Grandpapa struggles but he has taught me well. He says I remind him of father."

"Even so, your uncle and the governor will not trust the welfare of the settlement to a boy. You have grown up without a father and because of this you have taken on much responsibility and think of yourself as a man. In war, one mistake can cost the lives of many."

I began to argue but bit my lip instead, knowing they would not heed my words. Besides, if they heard the anxiety in my voice they would never let me help.

Once we entered the courtyard to the Castillo, Grandpapa took a seat.

Governor Zúñiga turned away from studying the entrance to the inlet that leads to the Atlantic Ocean on the gun deck and descended the steps to the courtyard. An anxious crowd waited inside the courtyard.

"Help me stand, Pedro," said Grandpapa. "I must show strength in front of the governor. The townspeople must know their soldiers are loyal and can be trusted to defend the city."

"Our Castillo," began the governor, "is the largest and strongest fort in all of La Florida. It is strong like a castle, with coquina walls twenty-six feet high and sixteen inches thick. Our fort is the envy of every settlement. Because of this, it is also a military prize for our enemies."

I interrupted and asked Grandpapa, "But France and our enemy England are thousands of leagues across the Atlantic Ocean. How does this endanger our Castillo?"

Grandpapa squeezed my arm, trying to steady himself. "Now that France and Spain have become allies, England is afraid we might conquer her territories in the New World. The English territory of Carolina is only a two-day journey by boat from St. Augustine. French territories border Carolina on the west and Spanish territories surround her to the south. We are the Spanish territory threatening her in the south."

"But other territories are not as strong. Why would she attack us?" I asked.

"It is because we are the strongest Castillo in La Florida that England must attack. If England takes St. Augustine, the rest of the Spanish territory will fall as well." Grandpapa turned back to the governor, as did I.

I searched the governor's face for any sign of worry, but saw none. He concentrated only on the crowd. What did his heart really feel, I wondered? Did fear consume him as much as the rest of us who knew what was coming? It was indeed the mark of a great man to keep the weight of this news to himself.

"Governor James Moore of Charleston," the governor said slowly, "in the English territory of Carolina, is organizing an attack on St. Augustine before the French and Spanish can act against him."

Nervous whispers broke out in the crowd. My heart raced. I looked at Grandpapa but his stoic face remained unchanged.

"The English will be coming by sea and by land. They seek to surround us," said the governor calmly.

Muffled groans erupted from the crowd. The governor held up his hands for silence.

"It is because of this I am ordering all citizens of the town to remain inside the borders of St. Augustine. Gather all foods. I am cancelling all leave for the soldiers. Reserve soldiers must report to the Castillo immediately. I order all colonists and Native tribes living in the small settlements neighboring St. Augustine into the fort. They cannot hope to defend themselves against an advancing army.

Pray to the Lord that our preparations are worthy."

A frantic crowd hurried from the fort.

Grandpapa Diego hugged me to his chest and held me tight. I closed my eyes. "I am still here, grandson," he whispered. "The Creator has not called me home, so that I too may face this trial. The time for you to be a man has come. Be strong. This is the greatest task our settlement has ever faced. We will embrace this together."

4

Preparing for War

Whoever is first in the field and awaits the coming of the enemy, will be fresh for the fight; whoever is second in the field and has to hasten to battle will arrive exhausted. — Sun Tzu

I TOILED IN THE GARDEN rolling pumpkins from the patch and picking rows of beans until every muscle in my body ached. Already this day, I had sharpened the knives, cut river cane for arrow shafts, chipped arrowheads out of chert, gathered nuts from the trees, chopped wood for the fire, and lay the corn in the field ready to be gathered. Grandpapa's words, "we must be prepared," drove me to exhaustion.

The air was thick with moisture. Miguel walked along the back of the house toward me, wiping large drops of sweat from his neck.

"My father leaves for Apalachee on a nine-day journey, sixty leagues west. The governor has ordered twelve soldiers to aid Capitán Solana in Apalachee so he can defend the town. Father says the governor fears the English will strengthen their position by attacking the missions supporting the Castillo. He is sending father with machetes and hoes so they can build a palisade around their mission. My mother fears my father will not return. She has not stopped weeping."

I laid my hand on his shoulder. "The governor must trust your father to give him such an important duty. I heard my uncle tell Grandpapa that the governor intends to ask the city of Pensacola for help, too."

A spark of hope ignited in Miguel's eyes. "When will help come?"

I sighed, knowing what I said next would not please him. "Not for many weeks. Pensacola lies one hundred and forty leagues west, a twenty days' journey."

Any hope Miguel had felt disappeared.

Then the sound of hooves hitting the ground caught our attention. We turned to see a horse and rider fly past with great speed on its way to the Castillo. We dropped everything and ran after the man on horseback. He rode through the entrance into the Castillo.

A large crowd hurried toward the entrance. The garrison blocked the path. Miguel and I pushed our way through the growing crowd toward the front, where I spotted a friendly face. The blacksmith's daughter, Margarita, talked privately with two men standing guard at the gate.

Like many of the townspeople, Margarita was of mixed heritage. Her father, a runaway from Carolina, was a former African slave and her mother was Spanish, making her a *mulata*. Her father sought refuge within Spanish territories when a previous Spanish governor had emancipated both Spanish slaves and African slaves owned by the English. He made his way to St. Augustine to become a free man and open a blacksmithing shop. The blacksmith, his wife and children, plus many other former slaves, were loyal inhabitants of St. Augustine. My friend Margarita was his eldest child.

When she had finished talking, I pulled her aside. "Pray tell, what has happened?"

Margarita's dark eyes filled with tears. "The English have captured the mission villages of San Pedro de Tupiqui, San Felipe, and Santa Catalina. Two Spanish guards have died protecting the island. The invaders sent flaming arrows into the missions, lighting the thatched roofs on fire and burning everything to the ground. Many children and people were lost. The English army is destroying every mission on their march to St. Augustine."

A lump formed in my throat. My heart pounded. I stared, eyes opened wide, at the restless crowd. I struggled to speak. "Those missions occupy Amelia Island! That is only a day's ride from here."

Tears streamed down Margarita's face. "The governor and his officials have been behind closed doors since noon. And now this new messenger arrives and he will report only to the governor."

People anxious for the news waited for the governor to come outside and speak. His absence sent frantic whispers rippling across the crowd. As more and more people arrived, the panic increased.

While we waited, a member of the garrison emerged from the gate. He moved with great haste toward us. "MOVE ASIDE! I must attend to official business." He pushed through the crowd, ignoring pleas that he speak.

I stepped boldly in front of the soldier and blocked his path. "Pray tell, what has happened?"

Stubborn eyes meet my glance, but when the soldier noticed the large crowd of anxious faces growing around me, he paused. "The governor is instructing the frigates, *Nuestra Señora de la Piedad y el Niño Jesus* and *La Gloria,* to carry messages to Havana. He is asking the governor of Havana to send their Spanish men-o'-war to protect St. Augustine, but it is too dangerous for our frigates to sail in such rough seas. On this very day, a storm approaches. Pray the weather calms so our frigates can set sail before the enemy arrives." Then he pushed his way past and disappeared from sight.

A dark blanket of clouds moved overhead. Large swells of water began to lash against the seawall but the full force of rain held back. Palm trees bowed toward the earth under growing winds.

Miguel tugged at my arm. He pointed at Father Francisco. "The Father summons everyone to the church."

I shifted uneasily. "But we must help secure the frigates. A storm will sink the strongest ship."

Placing his hand firmly against my shoulder, Miguel looked toward the sea where the anchored ships rocked in the water. "Surely that is the garrison's duty."

I drew in a deep breath before following my friend to the church against my will. Thunderclouds gathered overhead. Large, solitary raindrops fell from the sky. We pushed into the crowd of parishioners hurrying through the arched doorway, where they filled the pews and aisles. The wind began to howl. Babies across the room cried.

When the last parishioner passed through the door, Father Francisco raised his hands in prayer. Then he turned his attention toward the crowd. "Take comfort in knowing the Almighty has blessed us with news of an advancing enemy. The enemy had hoped to surprise the town of St. Augustine and to take us unprepared. England has lost her easy victory. We will pray that our preparations are sufficient and that our soldiers go with God's blessings."

An elderly man, gripping the back of the pew, stood. "But Father, how does the governor plan to attack the enemy with so few soldiers? Many are retirees or stricken with illness and the others are not well trained. Provisions of food and supplies from Cuba and Spain have not arrived for three months and our guns are too few."

Pushing my way to the front, I turned toward the restless crowd. "I am not helpless. Hand me a musket and I will meet the enemy in the woods!"

"Pedro," said Father Francisco calmly, "you are too young, my child. Only because of our great need has the governor lowered the fighting age of eighteen to fourteen, but he will not allow any younger to serve."

I opened my mouth to speak, but the Father raised his hand, silencing my voice. I bit my tongue instead to keep my words from escaping. It hurt, knowing I remained invisible to them. My dead father could not boast of my deeds or parade me before the garrison so they would know the man I was becoming. Again, was it that, or did they shun me because of something my father had done? Frustrated, I returned to Miguel's side.

"Be content, Pedro," whispered Miguel. "Your time will come."

Then the church doors opened and members of the garrison entered. The sergeant made his way to the lectern, where he turned to face the townspeople. "I am here to report that three English ships have been spotted sailing south toward St. Augustine. It will not be long before they enter the harbor."

These words spread fear across the room like wildfire. Chaos broke out. People rushed the doorways, the weaker trampled by the strongest. The garrison blocked the exits, forbidding anyone from leaving. Babies wailed as the sergeant and Father called for silence.

"Please, please . . . listen, my people," begged the Father. "God is our light. We have been given this news so we may prepare. But we must be calm."

Voices dropped to a whisper.

The sergeant pointed toward the Castillo. "The governor has ordered everyone to collect their valuables and bring them to the Castillo. Churches and shops are to remove everything of value so it may be used for building shelter. Fear not, you will have time to gather your things. When you hear three cannon shots and the bells start to ring, it will be time for the town inhabitants, nearby villagers, and tribes loyal to Spain to take refuge inside the Castillo. As soon as everyone is inside, the gates to the fort will be locked."

Silence fell across the room. The storm began to pound the walls of the church. Thunder cracked overhead.

Gripping her child tightly to her chest, a mother stepped forward. "But sergeant, our Castillo is too small for so many people. We will live in an open courtyard where the soldiers train to march. We will fight the cold and the rain, and winter is near. How are we to survive?"

"This is what God asks of us," answered Father Francisco. "Our hardships serve to make us stronger. With His guidance, we will find the strength, the wisdom, and the way. We must trust in him, my children."

"Why do we not defend the town?" asked a grandmother of many years. "We will be at the mercy of the English army if we sit inside the Castillo waiting for them to breach the walls. Surely, there is a better way."

Many nodded and I could no longer be silent. "Once we take shelter inside the Castillo, we can only defend ourselves. This does not seem wise."

The crowd murmured in agreement. Miguel nodded next to me.

The sergeant shook his head. "The governor has studied reports of the advancing army. With the fall of our outposts and missions in Amelia Island, we cannot hold the town. One thousand enemy soldiers approach by land and sea. Our two frigates, one hundred and eighty loyal Indians and blacks, and a couple hundred soldiers, many with little experience, cannot withstand such numbers. We must take refuge inside the Castillo and pray it remains strong until reinforcements come."

Miguel and I stared at each other, anxious about what was to come.

5

Under Siege!

*The supreme art of war is to subdue
the enemy without fighting.* — Sun Tzu

BEFORE MY GRANDPAPA'S MIND became mired in childish babble, he taught me many things about war and being a soldier. The time had come to share this knowledge with Miguel as we sat by the fireplace readying our weapons.

"Miguel, to be 'under siege' means the enemy intends to trap the townspeople and garrison inside the Castillo so we cannot move. The English will cut off any supplies coming into the Castillo so we have no food, no water, and no way to help ourselves. We will be forced to live on what we have. They intend to stop all messengers from riding in or out of the fort. If we are to win, we must outlast the enemy with soldiers, food, supplies and water. This is hard to do, because the enemy can come and go at will. Our enemy will have the control."

Miguel furrowed his eyebrows but said nothing. I slipped a finished arrow into my quiver and picked up another piece of cane to sharpen.

"Our garrison is able to the keep the enemy from getting close to the Castillo by shooting at them with our cannons and muskets. In order to win, the enemy must break holes in the Castillo's walls until they fall. They will use mortars that explode in midair and rain shrapnel down on the people."

I paused, my words forming a knot inside my throat. All my life I have witnessed the garrison defending the town, but I have never felt the weight of such words before. The sting was deep.

I swallowed. "To make all of this possible, the English will dig trenches so they can get close to the Castillo. It takes time and hard work to dig trenches leading up to the Castillo, but these paths will allow the enemy to win. They will dig out of range of our guns so we cannot shoot them. To do this, they will fill tall wicker baskets called gabions with dirt from the trenches. Then they will place the gabions on top of the ground to form a wall. This wall shields their soldiers from the garrison's gunfire. Next, when they have dug closer to the fort walls, they will bomb us. If the walls crumble under their cannon fire, we do not have enough soldiers to defend the fort. The enemy will overwhelm us and we will die."

Fidgeting uncomfortably, Miguel squeezed his hands together. "I will help any way I am able."

The knot in my throat did not lessen. Not wanting Miguel to see the worry in my face, I held the river cane close to my eye and measured the straightness of the shaft. "If that task is not possible, the English will try to enter the Castillo by digging a hole underneath the curtain wall. Or they will force our small garrison to use our short supply of ammunition by increasing their attacks. Or they will starve us and make us so weary that we cannot fight. Or they will trick us into a surrender or convince us we cannot win."

Miguel said nothing.

I looked away, knowing my words were heavy. "This is all part of war, Miguel. It is a matter of life and death, with only one outcome."

He drew in a deep breath. "There is much to consider, Pedro. Have you finished?"

I sighed. "The enemy may also use treachery by convincing a member of our own garrison to betray us. That is why it is important for the governor to keep the morale of his soldiers and the townspeople high so temptation cannot take root."

Miguel slid the sharp stone around the tip of his old quarterpike, sharpening the end to a fine point. "The last thing you say troubles me the most. I have heard much grumbling amongst the townspeople. They complain already and we have not yet been tested."

I tied an arrow head to the end of the cane shaft. "I worry as well. We do not know how long the siege will last or if reinforcements will come. The enemy will seek to starve the people, but our governor is experienced in siege warfare and will not allow this to happen, no matter how weary the people. Already, he orders our soldiers to fill the well in the center of town with sand. He robs the enemy of its easy access to fresh water."

Miguel looked toward the chapel. "My own stomach growls at the thought of little food, but I will pray for the people to have patience."

I cut into the end of a new shaft. "It troubles my heart to say this, but if the English breach the walls, we will be trapped like fish in a pond." Pieces of river cane fell to the floor as I shaped the tip. "The enemy knows prisoners will kill them if given the opportunity. And because prisoners will eat the food that is intended to keep the enemy alive, the English will sell the free blacks and slaves and murder everyone else."

Miguel looked up.

I stared into his wide open eyes. "Now you understand why surrender *is not an option*."

6

The Storm

By holding out advantages to him, he can cause the enemy to approach of his own accord; or, by inflicting damage, he can make it impossible for the enemy to draw near. — Sun Tzu

THE STORM THAT HAD BEGUN the night before continued to rage the next morning. Dark purple clouds blanketed the sky and the rain fell in sheets. Despite the impossible weather, people entered the Castillo carrying baskets, pots, trunks, and armfuls of goods. Many arrived by canoe.

By noon most had reported to the Castillo and settled into the courtyard. I counted townspeople, villagers, free blacks, freed slaves, and Indians loyal to the Spanish. The garrison, by order of the governor, calmly directed families and their belongings into different rooms of the fort and sections of the open courtyard.

The rain had slowed. Chickens ran loose, looking for shelter. Horses and pigs ran wild in the dry moat below the walls. The commander of the Castillo commandeered all food brought into the fort: maize, ground flour, ripe and unripe squash, figs, oranges both green and small, citron, sweet potatoes, pomegranates, and anything else that could provide nourishment.

To safeguard the supplies, the guards ordered all food stockpiled in the storerooms. Each family was to receive a daily allotment from their confiscated rations. The governor decreed that if the town survived, reimbursement would be paid to the farmers for their crops and animals later. But everyone, including those who came without food, would receive rations.

A young soldier, drenched from head to toe, directed our family to a place inside the courtyard close to the chapel. To the disappointment of many, the rain picked up again and did not abate. Sitting on top of the trunk, Grandpapa looked quietly around while rain dripped off his face. His mind drifted in and out of childish babble today, but his eyes told me he was aware of our quandary. His eyes seared me with an intensity I had not seen in a long while. It was as if he willed me to stay strong.

"Pedro, take your grandpapa into the soldier's quarters," said the approaching sergeant in a voice loud enough for all to hear. "Every solider is to report to duty. We voted to give him a bed under our roof. He is still one of us."

I breathed a sigh of relief, knowing the Almighty had spared my grandpapa from the cold ground and the biting rain. Grandmamma and I set his small straw mattress next to the fireplace in the soldier's quarters, where we stood and silently watched until he drifted off to sleep.

"How much does he understand today?" I asked.

"He understands some but his mind cannot reach us. I am confident he will find his way when the time comes. He always has," she said, patting me on the arm.

Grandmamma kissed Grandpapa on the forehead before we stepped back inside the courtyard. The howling winds lifted people's belongings into the air and out of reach. Baskets, articles of clothing, and bedding flew frantically through the air before sailing away. Thankfully, our spot close to the wall spared us the full impact of the wind and we lost only a worn blanket.

Miguel leaned into the wind, making his way toward us. "Pedro! The frigate *Nuestra Señora* struggles in the sea. She is trying to pass over the sandbar and into the harbor where *La Gloria* waits. If she cannot pass into the harbor, they are ordered to sink her on the rocks so she does not fall into enemy hands."

My heart quickened. "Then we must help!"

The wind whistled and the sky grew dense with dark clouds overhead. Running through the open gate, we pushed toward the seawall, where I fought to keep my ground and Miguel struggled to remain upright beside me. A deafening wind howled in our ears.

It was then we saw a great gust of wind hit the frigate broadside. The *Nuestra Señora* dipped far to her port side while three crewmembers climbed the mast, attempting to cut the sails free. Suddenly, the mast snapped in two. Our screams of horror fell flat inside the wind.

A man fell to the deck and the other two tumbled into the churning sea. The frigate tossed wildly back and forth in the raging waters, its huge mass weightless under such power. Then the wind caught hold of the ship and smashed it against the rocks as if it were a small wooden toy. The impact splintered the bow into pieces. The stern raised up bobbing in the water before following the bow slowly into the water. Within moments, the *Nuestra Señora* had vanished.

Clutching my arms in panic, I pushed to the edge of the rocks frantically searching for survivors. Only fragments of the *Nuestra Señora* churned in the surf. Large, pounding waves smashed wildly across the rocks, threatening to wash me under. I leaned to the side pointing at the rough sea. "Look!"

A boat emerged out of the spray, tossing back and forth in the choppy water. It dipped to one side but righted itself before falling under the waves. Some of the men used their helmets to bail water from the middle of the boat while others leaned in the opposite direction, counterbalancing the effects of the wind. Then the boat dipped to the other side before rolling back into place. A large wave smashed against the side, spilling another wall of water inside as it fought to move closer to shore. A second boat bobbed in the water behind it.

I stepped down on the lowest ledge with Miguel clutching my clothes from behind so I would not fall forward. The man at the front of the boat tossed a rope in the air, but the wind twisted it around and sent it flying out of reach. Again, the man threw the rope; again, it twisted in midair out of reach.

"Pray they do not break against the rocks!" I screamed. "They will float out to a murderous sea before we can seize them."

I edged slowly across the rocks, anxiously searching for anything to aid me in a rescue. A long wooden beam tossed back and forth inside the rocks. I grabbed at the slippery surface, fearing the sea would pull the beam and me out to sea. My hands slipped and it pulled away.

Panic set in. "Miguel, HELP ME!"

The current suddenly brought the beam close to the rocks

again. The end of the beam shot up out of the water. I hugged it to my chest and Miguel latched onto the middle. To my dismay, it yanked free of our grasp and smashed against the rocks again. My heart sank.

Little had I noticed a group of seven men making their way across the rocks toward us until suddenly a total of nine sets of hands lifted the beam up off the rocks when it came crashing in again. The men carried the beam back to the ridge where they angled it out so it jutted out from the shore.

The first time a longboat came within reach, a wave smashed the boat into the rocks, but the crew leaned back, forcing the boat to lurch sideways before being damaged. The next wave sent the boat sailing in a different direction. It twisted awkwardly in the water, almost sinking under the waves. Then the waves momentarily lessened and the crew hastened toward the beam, where the villagers helped pull them to safety. The crew from the *Nuestra Señora* came to rest safely on shore.

That night in chapel, Father Francisco said a special prayer for the two crew members who had been lost at sea.

7

The Enemy

Carefully compare the opposing army with your own, so that you may know where strength is superabundant and where it is deficient. — Sun Tzu

EXHAUSTION FROM THE STORM lulled me to sleep even though wet clothing and a cold ground served as my bed. By morning, my eyes opened to a large, blazing sun rising over a clear, blue sky. Next to me inside the courtyard, people lay side by side, still asleep. I stepped into the sunlight and stretched.

"Grrrrr . . . grrrr . . ."

My own stomach growled, but I knew that was not the source of the sound. Turning slowly around, I saw a large wolfhound pup lying next to its owner. It bared its sharp, pointy teeth directly at me. Averting my eyes, I stepped back and tiptoed slowly away.

"Pedro, fetch some water and then bring your grandpapa to breakfast," said my mother, unaware of the danger I faced.

The wolfhound eventually lowered its head and I grabbed the pitcher and walked through the many campsites toward the large well located in the southwest corner of the courtyard. Soldiers stood guard. One rationed out the day's water allowance. I waited in a long line for my turn.

"Good morning, Pedro. Your grandpapa awaits your visit this morning," said Sergeant Juan Felipe, a good friend to the family and member of the garrison bunking with Grandpapa in the soldiers' quarters. He poured water into the pitchers placed on the ground. "His mind is clear today."

My heart lightened. "And how was his sleep, Juan Felipe?"

"Last night, the soldiers told him how the sea claimed the *Nuestra Señora* for its own, and how his grandson helped save the crew. We do not know how much he understood but he nodded when we spoke your name. Restlessness consumed his sleep until the storm's thunder stopped."

I set my empty pitcher on the ground next to the well's wooden cover. Fortunately, the Castillo had three freshwater wells. The governor worried that if the wells ran dry, the townspeople would die of thirst and the English would claim an easy victory, hence the guards.

Crossing my arms, I looked directly at Juan Phillipe. "I must become a soldier. I have proven my bravery and the garrison is short on men. Will we not need to increase our ranks to battle the English?"

Juan laughed. "Pedro, you still have the body of a boy. It takes a strong back to move the cannons and load the ammunition, and you have not been trained to fight. The mind must be strong and not flinch during battle."

"I will not flinch, Juan! I am steady. Ask Grandpapa, he has trained me since I was old enough to hold a musket. And I am stronger than you think. I attend to the fields and build shelves and trunks for the store, and for the house. I am capable, Juan Felipe, and my heart is true." I waited expectantly for Juan to recognize my worthiness.

But Juan put down the bucket of water and placed a hand on my shoulder. "I am truly sorry, Pedro. If it were up to me, I would make you *capitán*. I owe that to your father. He saved my life more than once. He was my friend, and I miss him still."

The troubling thought that had plagued me for so long came pouring out. "Juan, when my father died in battle, were his actions true to the Crown?"

Juan's pinched face looked troubled. "Why do you ask me this?"

"The townspeople treat me differently from the other boys. Some keep their distance and the soldiers laugh when I talk of becoming a soldier like my father and my grandpapa. I worry that my father's actions in battle were not honorable and I am shunned because of this."

Juan measured his words. "I have heard rumors, but I do not believe them to be true. Do not trouble yourself with such falsehoods. I knew your father well, and know the man that died that day."

"What rumors? What do others hear?"

Juan stared into my eyes. "I will not repeat such lies and I will not fill the head of his son with false witness. If we survive this, we will discuss the matter further, but not now. The enemy is near and we must keep our hearts ready, not troubled by idle gossip."

As much as I wanted to press him further, I stared at the creases in his forehead knowing the matter would not go further. I sighed. "What does the governor plan for today?"

"Now that the weather has cleared, *La Gloria* will be free to sail for Havana," he said. "They ready our only ship for the voyage."

"What can I do to help?" I held my breath, anticipating his reply.

"For now, you attend to your grandpapa. He has served his country well."

"I am able to do more than help my family. Perhaps I may do things the garrison cannot?"

"All is being done, young Pedro. Do not concern yourself with such things."

He began to pour water into my pitcher when a guard rushed out of the San Carlos bastion watchtower. That is when I learned that in a time of war, a person must be able to shift directions just as the wind redirects its path.

"The English have arrived!" he shouted. "Three ships have passed the harbor and are heading toward the Matanzas Inlet where *La Gloria* waits to depart!"

Men who had been lying idle in their campsites jumped up from their beds and rushed toward the gun deck. Everyone had expected the enemy vessels to anchor outside the fort's harbor, just out of reach of the Castillo's guns, not travel farther down the sea to where *La Gloria* lay hidden from view.

Panic broke out in the courtyard where the view was limited to coquina walls and the sky above. Terrified faces pushed toward the gun deck, trying to move up the ramp where they could see the land surrounding us, but guards blocked the path. Juan Felipe pushed through the men and disappeared out of sight.

"*La Gloria* will not be able to sail. All is lost!" a woman wailed.

I moved through the crowd and out the open gate. Miguel pushed through the crowd to join me on the seawall. Fragments from yesterday's sinking of the *Nuestra Señora* lay wedged among the rocks.

Desperation consumed Miguel. He pointed to the three ships passing south along the sandbar. "The enemy has proven to be clever. They plan to block *La Gloria* from leaving! She will not be able to send for help and we will be stranded without reinforcements."

I pointed north. "Look. More ships?" The small dots visible along the horizon grew as I counted the numbers. "Ten more ships come!" I gasped. "Sloops, brigantines, and a man-o'-war!"

A feeling of absolute terror came over me. Miguel did not move.

Then we heard the sound of hooves pounding the ground and we turned to see two riders emerge from the Castillo going west at a full gallop.

It was then Governor Zúñiga summoned all to the courtyard. "My men report the English army has disembarked farther north and is on the march toward St. Augustine. Do not despair; our soldiers ride west to Pensacola. I have ordered the garrison in Pensacola to send a ship to Havana for help. I will continue to gather information and send out messengers until the enemy makes it impossible for me to do so. Go about your daily activities. The fort's gate will remain open until all of our neighboring inhabitants are housed safely inside the Castillo. I will wait as long as possible, but the time to lock the gate grows near. When you hear three cannon shots, and the sound of the bells, the gate will shut and the bridge will be drawn. At that time, anyone outside the walls will not be allowed to enter."

Then a small band of soldiers rode into the gate, dragging three captured English prisoners behind them.

8

La Gloria

All warfare is based on deception.— Sun Tzu

BEING TOO YOUNG TO FIGHT was not my only disadvantage. I was not privy to war strategy and information gleaned from English prisoners under interrogation. If it were not for Grandpapa living in the soldier's quarters, I would have died from frustration and a feeling of isolation. Fortunately, Grandpapa was privy to the garrison's actions, making him my eyes and ears.

Grandpapa leaned heavily against my shoulder as we exited the officers' quarters and made our way to our family-assigned space in the courtyard. The wolfhound I had encountered the day before bolted past us with a squawking chicken flapping in its mouth. A screaming *señorita,* her hand brandishing a knife in the air, chased the wolfhound through the crowd. Silence fell as the crowd watched. The wolfhound disappeared from sight.

Grandpapa chuckled. "A wolfhound will eat what is available. I'm afraid that *señorita* will eat no chicken this day."

I smiled. Grandpapa was himself today.

We had just settled into our seats when we saw Miguel making his way through the crowd. "Well? What did the prisoners say?"

Grandpapa waited until Miguel got closer, then he pulled both of us toward him. He lowered his voice. "Boys, actions made here today will have great impact on the war's outcome. Every decision carries great risk. We can only pray that we are able to outthink and outmaneuver the enemy. The enemy is the greater force. The words I speak are for your ears only."

I looked up, searching our surroundings for eavesdroppers. A group of children played a noisy game of knucklebones in the center of the courtyard. Others tended to their business. No one cared what an elderly man and two boys whispered against the wall.

Grandpapa's eyes grew wide. "The prisoners tell of a thousand soldiers coming by land and sea. The English have planned for a long siege. They bring three months' worth of provisions. The Castillo does not have that much food or ammunition, and reinforcements will take a long time to reach us."

I swallowed. The news was as grave as I feared.

Grandpapa shook his head. "The governor has sent some of our best soldiers to protect our lands to the west, the San Luis missions in Apalachee. We must protect ourselves from both land and sea. If they take Apalachee, all is lost."

Miguel drew in a sharp breath. Hearing that news and not knowing whether his father was safe in the Apalachee territory must have stung like a hot poker.

"Three canoes have been sent ahead to alert the Matanzas watchtower that *La Gloria* must set sail after sundown," he said. "Our survival depends on our ability to get help."

I drew back. "But three English warships wait outside the outlet for her," I whispered. "How can she pass them?"

"And ten more ships wait outside the harbor so she cannot leave in that direction either," added Miguel.

Grandpapa did not act as anxious as Miguel and I felt. "The three English sails have anchored in deep water on the other side of the island. We must have faith that Capitán Alonso will be able to maneuver around the enemy once the sun has set. Grandson, this is where you are needed."

I straightened my back. "Me?"

"Both you and Miguel. Two must attempt this task. The governor risks much with *La Gloria*. If *La Gloria* fails, the *capitán* will have no choice but to send her to the bottom of the sea where she will rot with the *Nuestra Señora*. If that happens, we have no hope of reaching Havana."

"What of help from Pensacola?" I asked.

"Official word is offering hope, but I fear help will not come. They say the ship they intend to send to Havana is in need of repair. She will not sail far before she is forced to return to dry dock."

I looked away. Help was not coming from the west. The English army was approaching from the north, and English warships surrounded our harbor. We had one frigate left. Any chance of help depended on *La Gloria* passing the three English ships after sunset or all was lost. This was a task of monumental importance. Suddenly I felt uncertain of my abilities. I felt small against the problems we now faced.

My hands began to shake. "What do you ask of me, Grandpapa?"

"And me?" asked Miguel.

"Tonight, you will distract the ships so *La Gloria* can pass unnoticed. Use the canoes hidden along the Matanzas riverbank from those who have taken refuge inside the Castillo. A waxing gibbous moon hangs in the sky tonight and it will offer only a small amount of light, making it harder for the enemy to see."

"And me," I reminded him. "I too will not be able to see."

"Nor me," added Miguel.

"Pedro, remember when I taught you to hunt deer at night? We waited in the dark until our eyes grew accustomed to the night. We learned that our night eyes will make out shapes and movement, but not the small detail we come to expect during the day. Your night eyes will grow once you have been away from the lights long enough. This will give you a distinct advantage over the enemy. Light from their lanterns shines aboard the English ships. Their eyes will not be adjusted to the darkness as yours will."

I hesitated before nodding. It would not be the same as using a torch or being outdoors during a full moon, but I knew the ground and sea well enough and would be able to find my way around. Grandpapa realized this.

"Fill as many canoes as possible full of dry leaves, pinecones, twigs, branches, logs—all that burns," he said. "You must pull the canoes upstream where they will float into the English ships when released. Ignite the dry leaves with your fire stones. Ships are made of wood. Fire is the enemy of a wooden vessel. You brought your fire stones from the house?"

"Yes," I said, patting my pouch. "I carry a piece of flint and steel with me always so making sparks for a fire is with me always."

I bit my lip, not as eager as before. Up until know, I did not doubt my abilities, but the lives of many depended on this. Surely a night watchman guards each ship. What if the fire does not light?

And once the first canoe is spotted, all three ships will take action. What if we are not able to escape in time?

I spoke my mind. "If I was asked to help, I did not expect to say this. This is a task of great importance. Someone more skilled than me should go."

"Does the governor order us to do this?" asked Miguel, his concern evident.

"No," said Grandpapa. "He trusts the *capitán* of *La Gloria* to find her way out. We must make sure the governor's plan works and help the *capitán*. I could not trust this plan to anyone other than you, Pedro. You know the woods and waterways better than anyone. You are able to move among the woods unseen at night. You have the skills of your father. You mastered the ways of making fire before you could reach the dinner table. This is something you can do, grandson. Sergeant Juan Felipe and I trust you do this. Only we know of this plan. We do not know where the enemy has ears and eyes and cannot risk it being known."

My mind held back. I did not want to consider the consequences of my shortcomings, but knew the battle could be lost because of me. That would be a cross I could not bear.

Grandpapa placed his hand on my arm. "Pedro, you have been called to action. I trust you to do this."

I bowed my head, heavy in worry.

It was Miguel who spoke next. "I am ready, Pedro. Tell me what to do."

Then I felt great shame at my hesitation. My city friend stood ready and able and I thought only of myself. Ignoring the doubt filling my head, I looked up. "When we set the canoes on fire, the ships will be distracted by the fire, and Miguel and I will have time to retreat."

Grandpapa nodded. "The three ships will pull up their anchors when they see fire floating toward them. They will not wait for embers to set them ablaze. While their eyes watch the canoes, *La Gloria* will pass downstream unnoticed. As soon as the sun begins her descent, you may leave the Castillo. We do not want enemy eyes watching us prepare."

I turned my eyes toward the gate, knowing our first test would be to pass cousin Nico on guard duty. He would alert the garrison and they would stop our exit from the fort before we began.

9

Sundown

Secret operations are essential in war; upon them the army relies to make its every move.— Sun Tzu

WHILE MIGUEL PLAYED KNUCKLEBONES with the others in the courtyard, I could think only of lighting fires with my fire stones. While I practiced creating sparks, Miguel threw a handful of sheep knuckles into the air. He caught one on the back of his hand and the others bounced off. The competition laughed at him.

"He plays like a *niño*," teased his opponent.

"I'm just practicing," Miguel said, grinning. "Take as many points as you can now. I will not yield later."

The competition continued to jeer. I joined their laughter even though troubling thoughts plagued me. What if scouts guard the shore . . . what if rough waters sink the canoes . . . . what if I drop my fire stones . . . . what if the wind blows in a different direction?

Overhead, the Castillo cannons fired.

BOOM!

BOOM!

BOOM!

The ground vibrated. The bell in the tower rang. Grandpapa had warned us beforehand what events were to come. "The governor signals the townspeople that the time has come to close the gates," I said. "He also warns the English that our guns protect the harbor."

The boys with the knucklebones rushed away. Screams of urgency erupted through the crowd. People from outside the walls hurried through the gate.

I shoved my fire stones in my pouch. "Miguel, we need to leave now. Cousin Nico will be busy with the crowd and cannot prevent us from leaving."

As I expected, Nico was busy assisting the crowd at the portcullis as they passed through the gate into the courtyard. Then a flaw in our plan occurred to me. A fort is made to keep people out and once the gate is down, Miguel and I would be barred from entry. My heart grew heavy. What else had I not considered?

When we reached the gate, my fear became real. Nico spotted us through the crowd and moved to block our path. But a man carrying an elderly woman and lugging a trunk behind him appeared at the gate. I breathed a sigh of relief when Nico was forced to help and I rushed Miguel through the middle of the oncoming crowd and out the gate.

My hopes at escaping without consequence were not to be. Cousin Nico's weaselly voice rose above the chatter. "Going back to collect your dolls? Does young Pedro lie awake at night because he cannot sleep without them? The drawbridge is going up and I will not let you enter after that!"

Knowing the confrontation was far from over, I shrugged off his continuing barrage of insults and disappeared into the streets where the neighborhood houses blocked us from view. Then we cut through the trees to the riverbank. Just as Grandpapa had predicted, dozens of abandoned canoes hid along the bank.

✳✳✳

OUR EYES ADJUSTED to the dimness of the night sky once the sun went down. We took off the extra tunics we had worn for the task and used them like baskets to collect all that would burn. We saw well enough to fill five canoes, but the task took us many hours to complete. The previous storm had left the ground wet with pools of water.

Soaked in sweat, Miguel straightened his back. "Gathering kindling is one thing, but the two of us cannot guide five canoes at one time."

I pulled a plant from the ground and held it close to Miguel's face. "We will twist ivy and grapevines into rope. Watch as I braid the vines and pray that it holds. These canoes are very heavy."

It took a great deal of time to crisscross vines into a brace and run the vines down the side of each canoe so we could connect them into a line. Next, we wove a thick woody vine to form a tow line from the lead canoe to the next canoe. The moon had moved high in the sky by the time we finished.

I walked the riverbank, surveying our path, when another flaw in the plan came to me. We and our string of canoes had to sail past the Matanzas watchtower and *La Gloria* on our way to the three English ships on the other side of the inlet. Our own soldiers might mistake us for the enemy.

I drew in a deep breath. Did Grandpapa think this through with a clear head or did his mind slip in and out of child's play this day? I stared at the ground, thinking of other paths to the ocean. The only other path was the harbor in front of the Castillo where the garrison would see us from the gun deck and where the enemy anchored its ships.

A knot in my stomach twisted as I prayed I would not regret my actions later. Stepping into the water, I pushed the canoe away from the bank and climbed in front.

"We must paddle as close to the riverbank as possible. Our silhouettes cannot show against the night sky," I whispered. "We would become targets."

We had not cleared the bank when the canoe jerked forward and lurched to the left. Miguel fell against the side. The side dipped down and water rushed over the side. Water splashed us from head to foot.

I glared at Miguel.

"I admit to only seeing others paddle a canoe," he said with great reluctance. "It did not look so difficult."

My reaction was not as calm as I would have liked. "Digging into the water with your paddle almost tipped us, Miguel!" Then I took a deep breath, slowed my speech, and concentrated on quieting my voice. "Switch seats with me," I said more patiently. "You sit up front where I can direct you. A paddle should never be jammed into the water like digging a ditch. It unsteadies the canoe. Dip your paddle into the water and pull back smoothly but with strength. I will tell you what side to paddle on."

Fortunately, he mastered the skill quickly because our lives depended on it.

The weight of the fire canoes tested every muscle in our bodies but we put our backs into it. To my dismay, we advanced up the river at a very slow pace. I continued to search our surroundings, looking for any sign of danger. The Matanzas watchtower finally appeared on the right, its wooden frame towering high above the trees. I signaled for silence as we floated quietly past.

"Either they sleep at their post," I whispered, "or they have their eyes trained only on the English. Fortune has smiled on us this time."

On the other side of the inlet, the English ships blocked the only path out to sea. We traveled unseen until we rounded the bend to where our own ship, *La Gloria,* hid. Silhouettes of soldiers moved along the deck of *La Gloria* as they prepared for departure. The crew worked in darkness, her lanterns unlit.

I swallowed. Two boys and six canoes would not be able to pass.

10

Who Goes There?

We shall be unable to turn natural advantage to account unless we make use of local guides. — Sun Tzu

"PEDRO MORENO?" asked a familiar voice from the deck of *La Gloria*.

The astonishment and stupidity in my voice betrayed me. "Who goes there?"

"It is Juan Felipe. I help prepare the ship. *La Gloria* is ready and waits for her opportunity to leave for Havana."

"The crew knew of our arrival?"

"I informed the watchtower that canoes would be passing. The crew and *capitán* do not know your identities, but welcome your assistance."

Both Miguel and I breathed a sigh of relief.

"Then we shall continue." I laughed silently to myself. Did Grandpapa not tell me about the watchtower and *La Gloria* because it was unimportant, or did he test my skills to go around them unnoticed? As he has done so numerous times before, I suspected the latter.

When we came in view of the open sea, we saw the three English ships blocking the exit. Their lanterns twinkled like stars above the decks.

We squatted close to the sides of the canoe and pulled our paddles slowly across the water. A crosscurrent tugged at our cargo, pulling it in the opposite direction. The twisted rope of vines rubbed against the rough bark, straining against the weight of the five canoes. I prayed to the Almighty that the vines would not snap. So much depended on a mission where so many things could go wrong. We doubled our efforts to paddle against the strong current.

The enemy sat idle in the water with anchors down. Soldiers shouted across the decks. I strained to listen to words I did not understand. My heart began to race. Had they spotted us? Did they prepare to attack? I looked behind us. Should we turn and run?

"They argue amongst themselves about *La Gloria,*" whispered Miguel.

"And how do you know this?" I asked.

"My grandmamma is English. She has spoken to me in English since I was born."

"And you did not tell me this?"

"I did not think it important."

"It is important when your enemy is English!"

"Shh! They'll hear you." He lowered his voice to a whisper. "The *capitán* of the smaller ship wants to move closer to the inlet to narrow the opening, but the larger ships want to stay in deeper water. They wait for orders. The crews are arguing. They cannot see on the other side of the island and do not know how many frigates we have or if there are guns protecting the inlet."

"Good. Let them think our inlet hides many ships. That gives us time to ready the canoes."

"What do you need me to do? I am ready, Pedro."

"Get in the water and cut the last canoe free. Push it toward me. As soon as you have cut it loose, go back and cut the next one free. I will light the fires as quickly as I can. Once the enemy sees a fire, they will not wait to react. We must work with God's speed."

Miguel floated the first canoe toward me. I pulled the fire stones from my pouch and rubbed the flint against the steel. Sparks fell across the dry debris. Some of the sparks went out, but many burned. A small flame grew inside. I released the canoe into the current. Miguel hurried with the next one.

Suddenly, a chorus of frantic shouts erupted on board the closest ship.

"They see us!" called Miguel. Within moments, the ship dropped a longboat into the water. "They come! Hurry, Pedro!"

Two more longboats dropped into the water. Men running toward the cannons shouted in full force.

My heart thumped inside my chest. My ears swelled with sound. I stared at the fire stones in my hands, the feelings in my arms and legs fading away. My breathing raced. I did not think such power could render me so helpless, but terror grabbed hold of my insides and would not let go. Paralyzed with fear, I could not move.

It became clear why they said I was too young to serve. It is the hardening of a person's soul as they pass through fire, to come out the other side, that matters. This was my trial. I had to pass through the flames or everyone inside the Castillo would perish. The price was too high. I felt faint of heart. I wanted to hide. I wanted to run. I did not want this burden. I was not a man. I was just a boy. A knot inside my throat threatened to choke me. I closed my eyes. That was when Grandpapa appeared inside my mind. He looked at me with eyes full of pride and smiled. He placed his hands on my shoulders, looked me directly in the eyes, and nodded.

I understood. My time had come. I swallowed the knot inside my throat. My soul calmed. My ears cleared. Slowly, a force I have never felt before rose up and took hold. Determination pushed away my fear. I struck the fire stones with such force a meteor shower of sparks ignited the night sky. Within moments, every canoe floated in the current toward the enemy.

Crack!

A bullet hit the side of the canoe, sending chunks of wood into the air. "Get down!" I yelled.

Instead of ducking safely into the water, Miguel rolled over the side and into the canoe. *Crack!* A bullet tore into the wood next to him. Another bullet splintered the wooden rim into shreds.

"Look!" I pointed into the distance. "The canoes! They burn like bonfires!"

Five roaring fires floated into the English ships. Winds blowing across the surface of the water fed the blazing flames. The longboats full of soldiers suddenly turned back toward the ships.

When I witnessed the majesty of the fire canoes, and the longboats in retreat, a childish impulse came over me. I regret to say I foolishly stood up and punched the air with my fist. "FLEE, YOU RED-BELLIED SCUM!"

I can say now that standing in the face of an armed enemy is not the wise thing to do. A sudden pain, like a hot blade, stabbed the rim of my ear as a soldier lifted his flintlock and took aim. Blood gushed down the side of my head. I dropped to the bottom of the canoe and stayed there.

It was then that the first canoe, engulfed in a roaring fire, slammed into the closest ship. Flames crawled up the side of the wooden hull. Embers danced through the air. *Whoosh!* The mast caught fire. The flames leapt across the deck to the sail of the second ship. The men manning the sail jumped into the ocean.

While the crew of the first ship took refuge in the water, the second ship struggled to move away from the flames and the third ship, untouched, hurried to pull up anchor. During the commotion, *La Gloria* moved quietly out to sea.

While the enemy dealt with the growing threat, Miguel and I paddled safely back into the mouth of the inlet, where we were saddened to witness the third enemy ship turn its prow toward *La Gloria*. We could only hope we had bought *La Gloria* enough time to escape.

11

Into Town

Ground which can be freely traversed
by both sides is called accessible. — Sun Tzu

AFTER PULLING OUR CANOE UP on the bank and returning to the abandoned neighborhoods of St. Augustine, I realized that a town draws its energy from the people living inside. A town without people is simply space cluttered with meaningless walls and furnishings.

Excited by our recent victory, I ran through the dark streets, jumping up and down, punching the air with my fists. I boasted about my desire to set canoes on fire all over again to Miguel.

My friend did not share my enthusiasm and stopped to punch me hard in the gut. "Once is enough," he chided. "We must survive the next battle."

I smirked, placed my hand over my affronted middle, and took his objection as a sign of our growing friendship. Miguel had grown more confident, more willing to embrace the unknown. The Miguel who emerged from our confrontation with the English ships was not the same boy who had stepped off the boat from Spain. Our trial by fire had let Miguel pass through the flames to the other side, too.

If truth be told, I dreaded going back to the Castillo, where my days involved shuffling through the crowd from the soldier's quarters, to the well, to the latrine, to the chapel for prayers, and back to my individual space, where every conversation could be heard. One minute the crowd in the courtyard was solemn, the next minute hysterical. Tempers frayed at the smallest provocation. And the small portions of food rations left everyone irritable. My own stomach gnawed as if forgotten.

Our journey stopped in front of Miguel's house, where we had planned to stay the night before returning to the Castillo during daylight. We lit the stubby candles of two remaining lanterns. I laid a handful of pecans, which I had found while gathering debris for the canoes in the woods, on the table. Miguel climbed the orange tree in the back garden and picked four ripe oranges from the highest branch.

We gave thanks for the food before us and pounded the nuts open with a stone. Miguel sliced the oranges with his knife and handed me a piece. I shoved it into my mouth.

"Ay yi yi!" I jerked back, cringing. "These are foul!" The sour taste filled my eyes with tears.

My friend laughed. "The fruit from this tree is only fit to feed to the animals. But they provide nourishment and that is what we seek." He bit his lip, smiling.

Drying my eyes against my sleeve, I snorted. "You could have prepared me."

"Yes, but that would have robbed me of watching you," he chuckled.

I punched him hard in the arm. He doubled over laughing. Whether our repast tasted good or not was unimportant. We now ate to live. Oh, how I had taken things such as Sunday dinner with the family for granted.

Miguel wiped his mouth against his sleeve before unhooking one of the canteens hanging on the kitchen wall. "I did not mean to leave this canteen behind. It belongs to my father. Come, we must sleep before the sun moves above the horizon."

We each took a bed. Stretching out on a straw mattress, no matter how lumpy, was a privilege I now cherished. The straw beneath my limbs helped erase memories of the hard Castillo ground and the troubles we now faced. Weariness soon lulled us to sleep.

✳✳✳

I AWOKE TO A ROOSTER crowing in the distance and a sound I did not expect to hear. A horse, or should I say horses, clomped noisily down the street toward our location, their nostrils snorting in the crisp morning air.

I nudged Miguel awake.

He blinked at first. I pointed to my ears and the direction of the sound. We gathered our things and crawled out to the balcony where we could see the street below. I imagined an English army of Carolinians, cutthroat Yamasee Indians, and black slaves marching into town toward us.

Instead, I saw two men on horseback standing outside the door of the neighboring house. Another set of scouts rode in behind them. Within moments, eight scouts on horseback chatted openly under our noses. Well-hidden and naively unafraid, Miguel and I eyed each other with excitement.

Miguel listened carefully, his face showing his concern about what he heard. He leaned forward and whispered, "They report Colonel Daniel has destroyed all of the Franciscan missions north of the Nombre de Dios . . . cattle ranches, farms, surrounding villages . . . all vacant. The scout who came with Daniels wants to know Moore's strength . . . he answers Moore's ship has sixteen cannons— eight- and nine-pounders . . . others have smaller guns . . . they have brought shovels, spades, and pikes to build trenches around the Castillo . . . Moore came with fourteen ships and forty canoes. Another scout reports Indians are coming by land with flintlock muskets, pistols, and short, curved broadswords . . . altogether there are between twelve hundred and fifteen hundred soldiers."

I drew in a sharp breath. "That's more than the thousand reported earlier. The governor must know about the true strength of our enemy."

Miguel moved closer to the edge of the balcony. "Shhh . . . one of the scouts says this is Moore's siege . . . it was not ordered by the queen. Many are uneasy about it. They do not understand why they have not been met with resistance. The army prepared for a confrontation. They think this may be a trap. They plan to search every establishment, every house, and every church before reporting back to Colonel Daniels." He waited for the reply. "Pedro! They are starting here. Now!"

The downstairs door opened.

12

Run!

On hemmed-in ground, resort to stratagem.— Sun Tzu

IN THE NORMAL COURSE OF A DAY, I map out in my head all the escape routes available to me. A hunter and a soldier must know their surroundings. A person must know, in case of danger, what is the fastest route to safety? Where is the safest place to hide? Where will the enemy go next? Where will the enemy attack? This day was no different.

"Follow me," I whispered.

We scooted quietly across the floor of the back balcony. I slid over the north wall away from the window where I lowered myself to the ground. Miguel followed. We crawled on hands and knees past the orange trees and stopped behind the empty chicken coup.

"Wait," whispered Miguel. "We forgot the canteen."

"Leave it," I said.

"No. It is my father's. The enemy must not benefit from it."

I sighed impatiently. "Then I will get it, you wait here."

Miguel put his hand out to stop me. "No, I will do it. It belongs to my family."

It wasn't that I did not trust Miguel. He had earned my respect several times in the past few days. It was the enemy I did not trust. "Then we will both go," I said.

He grunted his disapproval but did not prevent me from coming. We glanced through the kitchen window. What we saw next made the hair on the back of my neck stand up. Two scouts tore through the house, flinging trunks open, tipping braziers over, opening baskets, pulling the lanterns from the wall, pushing dishes off the shelf and tipping the contents of the cabinets over. They sorted through the broken pottery and shattered onion bottles on the floor.

One scout picked a silver necklace out of the debris and slipped it mumbling into his pocket.

Miguel's face grew red. "They found my mother's silver necklace hidden in one of the pots. She must have forgotten to bring it during our rush to the Castillo. It is an heirloom passed down to my mother from her great-grandmamma. She treasures it above all things. The scouts complain there is little of value in this poor town. Governor Moore has promised the soldiers they can keep what they find as payment."

The canteen hung close to the kitchen window.

Miguel pushed past me ready to open the kitchen door. "Go back to the Castillo, Pedro. I intend to take back my family's canteen and necklace."

I shook my head. "Are you loco? Winning one small battle has puffed up your ego like a wild turkey spreads its feathers. We need to leave now before the soldiers spread to the houses behind us and cut us off from the fort. Those trinkets are but small matters with what is at hand."

Instead of heeding my words, Miguel opened the kitchen door and lifted the canteen from the pegs. He turned and smiled, triumphant in his success. Then I watched in horror as a third soldier, unnoticed before, grabbed Miguel by the scruff.

A rational person would have run for help. They would have realized that eight grown seasoned professionals, scouts who had slaughtered their way into town, stood in the way of any reasonable rescue attempt. Scouts are generally well fed, chosen for being smarter than most, stronger than the others, and are reliable, expert trackers who pay attention to detail. These same men carried swords, pistols, daggers, and muskets at the ready. They rode on horseback and could travel anywhere that a person on foot could go with greater speed.

The first thing Miguel did was go limp; like a dog when it doesn't want to go any further. I don't know where he learned that trick but it was effective. The scout screamed and pulled at him, but Miguel lay on the floor with his eyes closed. The scout yanked Miguel's head up but Miguel kept his wits about him and did not react.

The others came down the steps to see Miguel's limp form sprawled across the floor. I could not speak English, but I understood their intent. The scouts waved their hands back and forth between Miguel and north of the town, a place where Colonel Daniel camped, no doubt. They intended to hand Miguel over to the colonel.

The first scout slung Miguel over his shoulder and headed for his horse. Miguel opened his eyes and looked at me. To this day I will never forget that look of horror. Those eyes drove me to do what I did next.

The scout traveled west through the streets. I ran on foot behind him, darting in and out of the houses, worrying that I would not be able to see him change directions. Much to my surprise, he did not ride with any sense of urgency.

It soon became obvious as to why. Standing before us like a majestic monument, was the most elegant house in St. Augustine— the governor's residence. It was good fortune that the scout did not know most of the governor's belongings resided in the storage rooms at the Castillo. Greed overrode the scout's greater sense of duty that day, allowing me time to make my grand move.

The scout dismounted, leaving Miguel tied to the saddle, and entered the house. Choosing the best method available to me, I picked a leaf from the garden, pinched a piece off the serrated edge, crumbled it in my fingers and dropped it into the scout's canteen that was hanging from the saddle. Then I removed the canteen and placed it on the ground where the scout would find it. It would not be long before the intense sun of La Florida would drive the man to thirst.

Once I was certain danger did not follow, I led the horse across soft ground and away from the neighborhoods, where I stopped to let Miguel go.

His reaction was to punch me in the arm, grinning. "I knew you'd follow! My worries were unfounded."

Of course, I punched him back. "You could have been killed, but we won't speak of that now."

A return punch hit me in the stomach.

I doubled over. "What? Are you loco? I just saved you!" He pushed me backwards but I did not fall.

"Why did you leave me tied up so long? What if the scout had come back? I wouldn't have been able to help. He would have captured you and then we would have both been prisoners."

I stood my ground. "It did not happen."

Miguel frowned. Then he pulled his canteen off the side of the horse and pulled a handful of jewelry out of the saddlebag. "The scouts are splitting the booty amongst themselves. They hide it from the rest of the army." He lifted his mother's necklace from the pile and held it up. "See, I told you I would take back what was mine."

I was not so impressed. "Fortune smiled on you this time, Miguel, but do not press her again."

Miguel slid the necklace into his pouch. "What did you put in that scout's water?"

"Something to help him remember the day he looted St. Augustine."

His eyebrows lifted. "How so?"

I shrugged. "My Timucua grandmamma knows herbs and medicines. I have picked many remedies for the townspeople under her direction. The leaf I picked from the garden is poisonous if eaten but it produces diarrhea if just a pinch is used. Twenty-four hours of diarrhea. He will not taste the pinch I put in his water, but it will be some time before he bothers anyone again."

Chuckling softly to ourselves, we slipped between the houses and made our way back to the Castillo.

13

BOOM!

He will win who knows how to handle
both superior and inferior forces. — Sun Tzu

FORTUNATELY FOR US, Nico was not on duty when we returned to the fort. Although the soldiers on duty were surprised to see Miguel and me standing on the other side of the fort, the corporal gave the order to lift the gate. That is when we learned our arrival had been one of convenience and the lifting of the gate had already been in motion. A group of soldiers carrying saddles scurried across the bridge and ran down into the dry moat where the livestock stayed.

"The English army has entered the town!" shouted a soldier from the gun deck.

Soldiers on the gun deck fired west into the neighborhoods where we had just passed. The soldiers who had gone down into the moat rode out on horseback toward our missions in the west. In the opposite direction, the San Carlos bastion's sixteen-pound cannon fired into the harbor; the grapefruit-size cannonball falling short of the English vessels. The enemy sat safely out of reach, dotting the horizon like birds on a post. The shooting increased. Rounds of artillery shot filled the air while clouds of gun smoke choked those near it.

Miguel and I reported to my uncle what we had gleaned from the scouts. Then we returned to our families in the courtyard. Before we could settle in, something happened to knock us off our feet.

CRAAACK! An unexpected blast erupted from the San Pablo Bastion in the northwest corner of the Castillo.

BOOM! I stumbled to my feet. My first thought—the English have just bombed the San Pablo bastion!

"Pedro," called my mother, her eyes filling with tears, "go

check on your grandpapa! He helps on the gun deck today."

Fear filled my voice. "How can Grandpapa be on the gun deck?" His days of physically moving about unaided had passed. Then I realized the soldiers must have carried him to his post.

Grandmamma frantically waved me toward the gun deck. "Many of the soldiers do not know the ways of cannon shot. They required your grandpapa's artillery expertise in loading the cannons. Go. Hurry!"

Miguel and I fought like mad hornets trying to push through a crowd on the ramp to the gun deck. If not for the sergeant clearing our path, we would have rotted at the bottom of the ramp.

When we finally made our way to the San Pablo bastion, the sight that befell my eyes darkened my heart. A dark, thick cloud of gun smoke blanketed the air. Grandpapa lay next to the wall, some distance away. Covered in a layer of black smut, he struggled to pull himself upright. A burned image lay lifeless behind the cannon. Four nearby soldiers writhed in pain.

I choked on my words. "Miguel, help me move Grandpapa to safety." We moved toward his frail frame.

Miguel's wide eyes combed the destruction. "What happened?"

I had no words to offer. Silence fell between us. Cuts and burns, too many to count, covered Grandpapa's body. Singed clothing hung from his bloody limbs. Blood dripped from a gouge below his eye. I pressed gently on his middle, trying to see if he suffered inside. He drew in a sharp deep breath but did not utter a sound. Grunts of pain grew around us.

"Have we been attacked?" I asked, praying the blast had not crippled his mind.

He pushed my hand away. "Your grandpapa stills lives. I was far enough away from the blast. It is those brave soldiers who paid the price of using an old cannon and that foul black powder."

"What do you mean?" asked Miguel. "Were we not hit by the English?"

"The blast was our own." Grandpapa slowly wiped at the black film covering his eyes. "That cannon is old. We have asked the Crown for new cannons but they do not send them, and the poor quality black powder that they send us from Cuba fouls the barrel."

The governor made his way through the gathering crowd toward us. "By God's grace you have been spared, Diego. How do you fair? Should I call the surgeon?"

"Do not worry about me, Governor." Grandpapa tried to pull his shoulders back and sit as straight as possible. "Our wounded soldiers have a more urgent need."

The governor bent down and looked him in the eyes. "The gunner, Juan de Galdona, is dead, two more will not last the day, but five others may survive their wounds, if God wills it. How did this happen?"

Grandpapa's words were slow in coming, but he managed them nevertheless. "That cannon is old. It is possible the men overloaded the barrel. They rammed the barrel with round shot, bar shot, and grapeshot, but if the black powder does not burn evenly, or too much is used, the cannon will burn too hot and blow up. Too much powder and a bad casting could cause a breach. As you know, Governor, many good men have lost their lives this way, and many of our artillerymen have practiced too little."

The governor squeezed Grandpapa's good arm. "An inspection will most likely prove you correct. Next time, Diego, when you say a cannon is beyond its years of service, we will use it as a fencepost or as a ballast for the ships, so temptation does not change our minds."

Once the governor was satisfied that Grandpapa was sound, he returned to inspect the bastion. Miguel and I helped Grandpapa to his feet. Despite his best efforts not to make any sounds, whimpers of pain escaped his lips. His wobbly legs buckled underneath his weight, but we held him by the belt and under the arms. Family members around us howled in agony as they stood over their lifeless loved ones.

"Take me to the wall, boys," said Grandpapa, his words choking inside his throat. "I must see this enemy for myself."

Careful of his burns, we strengthened our grip around his frail frame, lifted him gently up and crept slowly toward the wall.

His head shook. "I will not be surprised to learn that there was a crack in the cannon. A crack in the barrel would make that beast all the more dangerous."

Far to the west we spotted the enemy, well out of range of our gunfire. The cannons took aim with little effect. A long line of English soldiers marched freely in twos and threes down the narrow dirt road. Next to them walked Indians loyal to England. Behind them rolled cannons and wagons filled with supplies.

The San Pedro cannon fired, but the English army marched undeterred into north St. Augustine.

14

One Cannon Shot Away

*He who can modify his tactics in relation
to his opponent and thereby succeed in winning,
may be called a heaven-born captain.* — Sun Tzu

REPORTS CONFIRMED there had been a crack in the old cannon. Overloading the cannon with shot, a crack in the barrel, and the inexperience of the men had generated a fatal backfire. Many prayed in the chapel for the wounded to heal and for the souls that had been lost; others kept their mourning to themselves. Despite the tragedy that had befallen the fort, life continued as before.

"Come, Pedro. Your food is ready," called my mother.

She dished out a helping of *cocido*, a spicy bean and pork stew made from our daily ration of food. Despite my grim mood, the flavor of garlic and beans helped lift my spirits. It was not long before Uncle Manuel joined us for dinner. He huddled close to Grandpapa, where they spoke in whispers.

Both my mother and my grandmamma attended to Grandpapa's injuries the best they could and only when he allowed it. Poultices of herbs covered his wounds. To my relief and the relief of the family, Grandpapa had emerged from the accident clear-headed and in sound spirits. In fact, the tragedy and the threat of the siege had cleared his head of childishness. No matter how much pain he bore, we could not expect him to say so. It was not in his nature to complain, even when it would have been justified.

The irritation in my uncle's voice grew. "Our enemy, Governor Moore, appears to have boldly taken up residency inside the friary of St. Francis. The English headquarters will stand only one cannon shot away from our royal fort," snapped my uncle.

"This was to be expected," said Grandpapa. He sipped broth from his spoon.

My uncle shook his head. "Moore will sit at the end of the Castillo's cannon range, mocking us. Every cannonball will fall short of blasting him to Hades. He taunts us."

"He plans to intimidate us," interrupted my mother. "He hopes we will become disheartened and give up. He wants us to see him untouched inside his headquarters every day, while his men build trenches and threaten our lives by firing cannons at the Castillo. We understand what he is trying to do. He will fail, Manuel."

My uncle looked down. "If that were only so. I'm afraid our missions and the territory of Georgia are lost. Our Spanish troops have either been captured or are lost in the swamp."

Mother cupped her hands to her face in alarm. "I had hoped not to hear such things! May God watch over their souls. We must go to the chapel and pray for them."

"They were some of my best soldiers," said my uncle sadly. "I needed them here at the Castillo. We have failed at stopping the army from overwhelming us. This news is hard to bear."

"And Miguel's father?" I asked. "Is there news of him?"

My uncle put his hand on my shoulder. "I am afraid there is no news, Pedro. We will go to the chapel and pray for him as well for the others. Tell Miguel he must remain strong."

I stared at my shoes. This news would be hard for Miguel and his family to hear. I could already feel Miguel's worry and hear his mother sobbing softly to herself.

"Governor Zúñiga is ordering all the houses closest to the Castillo burned down. These houses block our path to the enemy," said my uncle.

"We must burn our own houses? But where will we live?" gasped my mother.

"We cannot stop the enemy if they use our own houses for protection," answered my uncle.

Grandpapa patted my mother reassuringly on the arm. "Maria, surviving the siege first is all we must consider. The enemy has great strength. Houses are but sticks and stones." He turned toward my uncle. "When does the governor plan to set fire to the houses?"

"He will give the townspeople time to remove their belongings. We will then send out a sally of brave men and musketeers to torch the small and large houses closest to the fort during the night."

Grandmamma, who had been quiet up until now, took hold of my arm. "Pedro, I am in urgent need of herbs from the woods. Can you fetch these for me when the gate opens?"

My mother sat up. She looked at me and then at Grandpapa in alarm. I knew she worried for my safety, but would not object to Grandmamma's request. Grandmamma's needs were great and Grandpapa's wounds serious. I saw how it troubled my mother to remain quiet.

I took this as a sign that I may go. "Miguel can accompany me."

Wishing to keep our conversation within our own circle, my uncle motioned for us to move closer. "I need everyone's help on another matter," he whispered. "The governor has freed all the prisoners except for the three English soldiers."

"How can this be wise, Manuel?" asked Grandmamma.

"We cannot watch so many prisoners during a siege. Zúñiga has granted them full pardons and they have been released. The military fears the prisoners will escape the Castillo and give away vital information. The governor is especially interested in keeping an eye on the pirate Andrew Ranson. Many have forgotten that he is an Englishman."

Craning to see above the crowd, I searched for any sign of the prisoners but saw none among the many familiar faces. I knew every prisoner by sight, but none resembled the pirate. Ranson had been a resident of the Castillo for sixteen years. History says Ranson and Capitán Jingle had led a convoy of pirate ships along the coast raiding the Spanish in La Florida. Then he came ashore with some of his men in search of food and water and looking for ways to attack St. Augustine. When he saw a messenger leaving the fort, he captured him and learned about the fort's defenses.

But a group of cattle ranchers saw the pirates come ashore. They found the boat and sank it with their hatchets. Then, fifty Spanish soldiers emerged from the fort and captured Ranson and his group of pirates.

Ranson was tried and sentenced to death by garroting. The executioner twisted the rope around Ranson's neck, choking him as ordered by law. Ranson collapsed after six twists of the rope, but when the executioner twisted the rope one more time, it ripped in two and the pirate fell to the ground. When the friars examined the body, they discovered Ranson still lived.

The friars declared Ranson's survival a miracle and that he must be given sanctuary. The governor ordered the soldiers to garrote Ranson again, but the friars promised God would bring down his wrath on the garrison if they tried to undermine the miracle he had provided.

Communication and clarification on Ranson's case traveled back and forth between St. Augustine and Spain for years. In the meantime, Ranson learned to be a cabinetmaker. Not only did he work at the Castillo making cabinets, he acted as a translator for English prisoners. That is why Andrew Ranson was dangerous. He knew the inner workings of the fort and had every reason to betray his captors.

Not finding Ranson's face among the crowd, I lowered my head back into the closed circle.

My uncle suddenly stood. "It is time for me to return to the gun deck. The troops that the governor sent out two days ago are returning."

Grandpapa pushed at my arm. "Follow your uncle, Pedro. This will be a sight to behold."

I did not know of what he spoke, but my uncle smiled as he made his way through the crowd with me trailing behind. We turned toward the west. I will never forget what I saw next.

The enemy had continued to arrive for days. A long line of men on foot, horses, and supply wagons stretched from the surrounding woods to the town. But something else this day drew the Castillo's attention.

BOOM!

BOOM!

The San Pedro cannons fired on the enemy, having little effect but disrupting the orderly arrival. When the smoke cleared, we saw objects moving along the horizon. The objects ran toward the Castillo. I ran to the curtain wall to see what approached.

Within moments, a stampede of cattle came into focus, their great swarming mass moving toward us with hooves pounding like thunder. Weaving in and out of the outer rim of the herd rode a troop of men on horseback, their whips snapping wildly in the air.

Spooked by the Castillo's gunfire, the cattle tried to turn away, but the ranchers and soldiers forced them forward with whips. The cattle zigzagged right, then swerved to the left, galloping at full speed. The thrill at seeing our troops driving a herd of cattle through enemy lines was a sight to behold. But the best was yet to come.

The English did not have time to react. Before they could load their flintlocks, the herd tore through the enemy line. Frightened horses reared in terror, throwing riders to the ground. Wagons broke into splinters, their goods trampled into dust. Cannon carriages smashed to pieces as their heavy guns toppled over. Soldiers ran for their lives. The stampede moved as a sea of destruction, scattering the enemy into total chaos.

"BRAVO! BRAVO! BRAVO!" shouted the soldiers on the gun deck.

Cheers filled the Castillo as the garrison drove 163 heads of cattle safely past the enemy line and into the Castillo's dry moat below.

15

Into the Lion's Den

Opportunities multiply as they are seized. — Sun Tzu

MIGUEL AND I PASSED a string of horses prancing back and forth in a narrow section of the courtyard. Pushed to the side, people watched as the horses maneuvered. Grandmamma busied herself pulling on our tunics and brushing hair from our eyes.

It took the lifting drums on the drawbridge fifteen minutes to lower the counterweights into place. The small crowd surrounding us waited nervously for the wooden bridge to lower. I repositioned my axe inside my belt, pushed my bow into place, rearranged my quiver of arrows, and shook my canteen to make sure it was full. Miguel took his knife out, checked the sharpness of the blade, and tucked it back inside the sheath. He held his quarter-pike in his right hand. I smiled. This reminded me of our times before the war, only we were boys then.

"Remember to look for cherry leaves that are still green and search for willow tree bark that is not blemished. If you are able, pick yaupon holly too," instructed Grandmamma. She slid a large pouch across my shoulder. "Be very careful, Pedro. The enemy fills the woods. Guts are important. Your guts are what digest your food, but your brains tell you which things to swallow and which not to swallow. Beware of your surroundings and be wise in your decisions. I would not ask this of you if your grandpapa did not risk becoming worse without it."

Drawing in a deep breath, I willed my hands to be still as I slowly exhaled. "I am not afraid. My heart races, but my head is calm. Do not worry, Grandmamma. We will be very careful."

Miguel jabbed me in the shoulder with the side of his quarter-pike. "Do not fear, Señora Leena. I will take care of him."

I nudged him with my elbow. "And I will make sure the enemy does not carry you away."

The corners of Grandmamma's lips turned up, but her pinched brows did not relax. "Youth does not realize the danger that it faces. Your grandpapa bids me to trust in you, and I will do as he says. We must allow you to find your own way, but my heart does not feel any comfort in those words. Words will not shield you from enemy fire."

Pulling her close, I wrapped my arms around her for a long time. She squeezed back with a strength I did not know she possessed. Afterwards, I squared my shoulders, drew in another deep breath, and turned toward the drawbridge.

It was time for the families living in the houses closest to the Castillo to retrieve possessions that would be lost forever once our soldiers set fire to the houses. Miguel and I knew the musketeers on the gun deck would take aim at the enemy inside the town in order to protect the families as they ran, but not us. We traveled in the opposite direction and did not want to alert the enemy to our journey.

My foot tapped anxiously against the dirt as I waited for the slow clank of the drum chains to finish. My legs ached to run and my mind begged to be free. Confinement inside the fort made me feel like a trapped animal. When the gate lifted, I barged through the crowd and onto the bridge, where I slipped into the moat and ran north toward the marsh. Startled livestock scattered everywhere.

CRACK! CRACK! CRACK!

Musketeers fired into the air, covering those leaving the fort. Within moments, we had shimmed up the opposite side of the moat and stood at the marsh's edge, where we witnessed the others disappear into the streets behind us.

"The cattails and grasses in the moat will cover us. Give me your quarter-pike so I can find a path," I yelled over the gunfire.

Miguel reluctantly relinquished his precious quarter-pike. I poked the ground looking for firmer ground. Walking, or should I say trudging, through a salt marsh is slow going, but the vegetation offered concealment, making our journey possible. Gunfire continued to erupt from the fort. We emerged on the other side of the marsh unnoticed. I hesitated while listening to the sounds of the woods. Confident in the silence, we continued.

Once we were out of sight, I took in a deep earthy breath. "Smell that," I whispered. "The air is fresh, not like the Castillo where it smells of horse manure."

"Be thankful we have a fort for protection," scolded Miguel. "And give me my pike back."

I tossed the quarter-pike back to my grumpy friend. I did not hold it against him that he did not appreciate nature the way I do. To him, the Castillo offered safety, a place to hide, a place to be with his family. To me, it was a stone prison pinning me inside a coquina cage.

We moved deeper inside the woods. Evidence of the enemy's passage lay before us. Crushed plants and broken branches outlined a trail cutting through and around the trees. Hoofprints and deep wheel ruts covered the mud where smashed clumps of horse dung mixed with the dirt.

"This way," I said, pointing.

"Our enemies are many," said Miguel pointing to the numerous footprints. "The wheels carry something heavy. The ruts are very deep."

I patted him on the back. "Your tracking skills improve. A cannon has passed this way. The distance between the ruts is narrow compared to a supply wagon. Cannons weigh thousands of pounds. See the footprints on the outside of the ruts where the men guide the wheels and the hoofprints on the inside of the ruts where the horses pull it. Walk lightly; we do not know where the enemy hides."

I was relieved to see a cherry tree in the near distance. We made our way toward it, stepping over cypress knees and soft ground. Pools of water gathered on the path but a patch of dry ground appeared on the other side. The tree grew in an area of high ground and strong sunlight.

I hurried, gathering leaves and storing them inside the pouch. Not far from the cherry tree grew a willow tree. I took my knife and cut around the bark in a square. Then I pried it off with the tip of my knife, being careful not to expose too much of the bare trunk underneath. I did not want the tree to become infected or die because of my greed.

Miguel scanned the woods while I worked. The red berries of the yaupon holly stood out against the green and brown colors of the woods, making it easy for me to find. I picked as many leaves as I could as quickly as possible. The pouch I carried bulged with all that I had collected. Then I noticed the ground was covered in nuts. Knowing it was wise not to leave food behind, I placed a handful of nuts on top of the contents inside my pouch and shook. Many of them fell into the small gaps until the pouch could hold no more.

Miguel pinched his face in concern. "Pedro, I think something happens in the east. A flock of turkey vultures circles overhead."

I looked at the sky. Turkey vultures circle in large numbers when something disturbs their nesting area. I brushed the layers of pine needles on the ground aside and pressed my ear to the surface. Heavy equipment and animal or human movements make vibrations that carry across ground. I heard nothing.

Knowing that vibrations carry better in water, I eyed a large puddle we had just passed. I stared at the green water covered in slime and insects. Not desiring to stick my ear inside mosquito-infested swamp water, I walked away.

"There is nothing to hear. Perhaps the enemy cut down the turkey vultures' trees for shelter. We are safe for now. Come, I want to see if the mission has been captured."

Unfortunately, my declarations brightened Miguel's mood and we felt a false sense of safety as we started walking north. The problem, as I see it now, was my own foolishness at underestimating the enemy and Miguel's trust in me as his teacher. If he had challenged me, I might have rethought my decision. But as it was, I did not consider all that I should, and we walked boldly into enemy territory.

16

Into Enemy Territory

When you surround an army, leave an outlet free.
Do not press a desperate foe too hard. — Sun Tzu

MIGUEL AND I STOPPED behind a thick patch of trees, where we drank from our canteens and applied wax myrtle ointment to our exposed skin. A small swarm of mosquitoes hovered nearby waiting for any warm-blooded animals.

The Nombre de Dios mission, where the shrine of Our Lady of La Leche stood, and a church big enough to hold two hundred people, was located just north of the Castillo. The mission traced its roots back to 1565 when Admiral Pedro Menéndez de Avilés first came to the La Florida coastline and founded St. Augustine. Father Francisco López de Mendoza Grajales had performed the first mass on this hallowed ground and the Spanish settlement revered both the mission and holy shrine as sacred.

I knew we took a great risk in approaching the mission since the enemy had taken up residence in every available structure, but the garrison needed news of the enemy. "Miguel, do you promise to listen to me and do what I tell you to do so we not fall into enemy hands."

"I make no promises, Pedro."

I folded my arms and stared at him. Had I made a mistake in asking for his help? I pulled his arm. "This is serious. The enemy is not benevolent. We are a threat. They would interrogate us the same way the garrison interrogates the English prisoners. And that is not all that they would do."

Miguel grinned before punching my arm. "Do not worry, Pedro. We will do this together. This is my battle just as much yours. I too have family and loved ones in the Castillo. I do not plan to sacrifice you or myself to the English."

I punched him back, only harder. "Then keep your head about you and don't do or say anything foolish. If we are captured, act like you have the mind of a child and do not let them know you speak English. They must see us as worthless."

"Yes, *capitán*," he said mockingly.

We moved east toward the mission, stepping through the trees with great caution. I stopped periodically to listen to the sounds of the woods but heard only the fort's musketeers in the distance. The mission appeared through the trees. Three horses stood tied to a post out front. To observe the enemy and get away as quickly as possible was our only chance of survival.

"The governor was correct in his assessment. The English have set up camp inside the mission," whispered Miguel.

"This is indeed bad news," I said looking around. "They can see the Castillo's north side from here. The enemy now watches us from the north, east, south, and west. We must report back to the governor."

I turned to leave, pulling on Miguel's arm in an attempt to make him follow me.

He dug his feet into the ground. "We are close to the enemy and must look inside the window first. The garrison is not here so we must be their witnesses."

He, of course, was right. Going against my better judgment, I could not help feeling regret at hearing words I should have spoken myself. The front door to the mission opened. A soldier stepped through the doorway and placed a letter inside the saddlebag.

"We need to know what that messenger placed inside the pouch," whispered Miguel.

"There are three horses, so we must assume there are three soldiers. They will be able to see us through the window. We need to create a distraction first."

"What do you plan?"

I bowed my head in thought. What would make the enemy leave their post? Gunfire would get their attention, but I did not have a musket or pistol. It was too wet for a fire and I did not want to risk damaging the sacred mission unless it was our only course of action. I smiled. A simple solution occurred to me.

"I will shoot arrows at the door," I said. "They will come out to investigate. That means I will have to draw them out into the woods, which will leave you alone to look inside the saddle and take the letter. You read English, can you not?"

"My English grandmamma taught me well," Miguel stated while pulling something from his pouch. "That is too dangerous. I have a better idea."

I stared at the slingshot emerging from his pouch. "Where did you get that?"

He grinned. "I made it. I had one just like it in Toledo, where I practiced every day in the orchard. I can hit an orange at one hundred paces. I once hit the stained glass window in the church and shattered it into pieces. My father took my slingshot away until I polished pews and washed walls inside the church for two months. After that, my target practice was limited to hitting oranges and lemons inside the orchard."

His eyes sparkled. I saw Miguel with new eyes, wondering what other skills he might possess. "How come you have not mentioned your slingshot before?" I asked curiously.

"Because I have been the pupil and not the teacher. You have been teaching me the ways of the New World and I have been eager to learn." He pointed to a large tree on the other side of the mission. "If I hit that tree with a rock, do you think it will be enough for all three of them to leave the mission?"

I looked from the tree to the mission. "No. They will send one person. We need to build a large enough diversion farther into the woods so they all come out to check. We'll bundle branches and logs together and set them on a tree branch, and you can knock the bundle out of the tree with your slingshot. It will make a loud crash when it falls and all three of them will come out to investigate. Can you stand on the other side of the mission, where it is safe, to do this?"

Miguel smirked and I took that as a yes. We found the perfect tree and took great pains not to make any sound while we wedged branches with dry leaves still attached on top of a large tree branch. We selected branches with the largest dry leaves so they would rattle and make lots of noise when they fell. We needed the enemy to think the worst.

Miguel worked silently, placing branches carefully in the pile. I, on the other hand, was in a hurry and let a branch slip. It tumbled off the top of the pile, pulling a couple of other branches with it. They rattled, scraping the tree trunk on the way to the ground. My heart pounded inside my chest. I hid behind the tree trunk and Miguel squatted behind a group of bushes.

A soldier stepped out of the door and looked around. He studied the tree, unable to see the bundle hidden by the branches. His head cocked to the side, searching. Then providence smiled on us and a squirrel hopped across the treetop overhead, making the leaves rustle as it ran. Seeing the squirrel hop to a second tree, the soldier shrugged and returned to the mission.

Miguel and I stepped back out into the open and finished our job with great haste. Moving carefully to the other side of the mission, we found the perfect place to stand.

"I carry stones inside my pouch, but we need something bigger and heavier," said Miguel.

I surveyed the ground. Large, heavy pinecones lay among the pine needles.

"Can you sling this?" I handed him one.

Miguel took it in his hand and felt the weight. Then he placed it across the pouch of his slingshot and let it drape by the strings. He lifted it above his head and slung it around in a circle before bringing it back down without releasing it.

"I need a couple of practice shots," he said. "It has an odd shape that does not balance as it should. I fear it will not fly straight."

"Can you aim between those trees?" I pointed to a pair of trees in the distance. "It will land on ground soft with pine needles and it should not make too much noise because it is far enough away."

Miguel slung the pinecone quickly over his head several times before letting go. It bounced off the tree to the right. The second pinecone bounced off the tree to the left. The third pinecone ricocheted in between the two trees and fell on the ground between them.

"I do not like the feel. These pinecones are not dense enough and they do not land with the same force. I cannot spin it fast enough to gain as much traction. I do not guarantee it."

Then a thought occurred to me. "Come. I know where we can find what you need."

We pushed through the trees until we passed the dunes and walked out on the beach. Large, rolling ocean waves rolled across the sand to our feet. It wasn't long before we spotted chunks of coquina scattered along the sand. Miguel stopped to weigh each chunk in his hand before slinging it over his head and bringing it back down.

"If I cannot measure the distance the stone travels, it will not work. A slingshot works because of the speed at which the blow is delivered to a mark," he said.

After Miguel selected five perfect coquina stones, we headed back toward the mission.

17

Into Enemy Hands

He who knows when he can fight and
when he cannot will be victorious.— Sun Tzu

I LEARNED THIS DAY that you cannot control everything. Life and events happen no matter how much you plan and organize. Only a fool thinks otherwise.

Miguel's skill with the slingshot was impressive. I have to admit I felt some jealousy at the skill with which he handled his weapon. I had not learned to use a slingshot because I had a bow and axe at the ready. In my ignorance, I thought the slingshot to be old-fashioned and a lightweight tool, not worthy of exploration. The *padre* would point out later that David brought down the giant Goliath, not with a bow, or a sword, or an axe, but with a slingshot and a stone to the forehead.

I drew in a deep breath, anticipating the trial to come. "As soon as the soldiers step outside the mission, you, Miguel, take the letter from the saddlebag, and then follow me into the woods. This will give us enough time to get across the marsh and into the moat. We cannot expect protection from the Castillo."

I calmed my thoughts and steadied my hands. Miguel looked down, shaking his hands loosely beside him. Then we looked at each other, knowing the time had come.

Miguel removed the roundest chunk of coquina from his pouch and placed it in the middle of the slingshot. He balanced it before bringing it up over his head. He spun it around and around and around, then let go.

THWACK!

The coquina delivered a hard blow to the top of the bundle but the vines holding the branches together did not break free. He readied his slingshot again. This time, the second stone hit the center of the branches but the bundle stood. The third stone broke the binding free and the pile of logs hit the ground with a loud crash.

Three soldiers ran out of the mission. To our surprise, the scout that had captured Miguel in St. Augustine stood among them, penance for losing his prisoner, no doubt. Two of the men rushed toward the source of the noise, but our scout stopped to inspect his surroundings. Then he joined the other two around the corner out of view of the horses.

To my surprise, Miguel ran quietly toward the horses. They snorted and whinnied, anxious about the commotion and the appearance of a stranger, but Miguel's skill impressed me once again. He whispered to the most agitated horse and stroked its head. When it calmed, so did the others.

I edged around to the other side of the mission to watch the enemy. They stood over the pile of logs and pointed to several places in the woods. Our scout began to search the ground around the tree. I crept back to the other side waiting for Miguel to join me, only he did not come.

Moving toward the edge of the building to see why he lingered, I witnessed my friend sawing the horse reins with his knife, and as soon as that strap snapped in two, he started in on the saddle's girth! Desperately trying to remain calm, my heart churned anxiously inside my chest while I tapped my foot impatiently on the ground. Gritting my teeth until they ached, I proceeded to watch him cut the reigns and saddle strap of each horse.

When I crawled back to the other side of the mission to check the progress of our enemy, the scout had started walking toward us, his eyes slowly reading the trail to our present location. It would be a matter of seconds before he found us.

I had only time to scream, "Run!" before disappearing into the woods.

Within seconds, Miguel fell in behind me. We were victorious in clearing a blockade of fallen trees left by the storm, but our path took us through layers of fallen leaves and dried palm fronds. Breaking branches and crunching debris alerted the enemy to our direction. We had no choice but to make haste toward the marsh and worry about the consequences later. My ears throbbed with the thumping of my heart. My lungs burned.

Then the unthinkable happened.

I tripped over a ditch, somersaulted through the air, and landed on my back. The pouch of herbs flew through the air out of sight. My axe slipped from my belt and my bow snapped in two under me. The quiver of arrows lay scattered beside me.

Holding his quarter-pike tightly in his hand, Miguel leapt over my sprawled body and kept going. I tried to lift my head to see if he reached the water but my eyes would not focus. Then a grimy pair of hands pulled me from the ditch, flipped me over, and pinned me face down on the ground. Grandmamma's pouch lay within reach.

Two Englishman and a Yamasee Indian stood over me, arguing. Native to La Florida and Georgia, the Yamasees turned against the Spanish in favor of the English Carolina colonists. Both the Yamasees and Carolinian colonists were conducting slave raids against the Spanish-allied Indians and killing those that had no monetary value. A Spanish boy, such as me, was the later.

Consumed with fear, I spit the dirt from my mouth and listened to unknown words filled with hate. During my life, I have been in danger many times, but to be held captive by murderers who held no regard for life rendered me helpless. My heart pounded wildly in my chest. My mind raced with such speed that I feared unconsciousness. My whole body broke out in sweat.

Suddenly, the Yamasee hovering over me yipped and fell to the ground. He eyed the marsh and tenderly touched a bump growing on his forehead.

Swoosh! Thwack!

The scout hit the ground.

Swoosh! Thwack!

The third man fell backwards and did not move.

Miguel shouted from the edge of the marsh. "Hurry, Pedro, run!"

I struggled to my feet. Gathering my pouch and axe, which were close by, I turned toward the marsh and began to run. My wobbly legs threatened to buckle beneath me but I pushed through the dizziness. Aiming for the middle of my blurred vision, I prayed that the marsh lay ahead as the path continued to move up and down under my feet.

The Yamasee lifted his head and let out a high-pitched yell. More men poured out of the woods. Miguel moved out of the cattails, his slingshot spinning over his head. *Swoosh! Thwack!*

I entered the marsh. Miguel squatted, swinging his slingshot with formidable speed. His eyes found its mark and the stone from his slingshot followed. He stopped when I seized his shoulder to steady myself. Holding the pouch close to my body, we wove in and out of the tall marsh grasses, intent on confusing the enemy. Our lives depended on a small amount of cloth, a dwindling amount of stones, and trickery.

But the enemy was not so easily fooled. They entered the reeds behind us. Miguel turned and took aim.

Swoosh! Thwack!

A surprised Yamasee yelped in pain. We pushed ahead but the enemy was faster. Miguel stopped every few paces to take aim. No matter how fast we moved, or how many stones Miguel delivered, the enemy kept advancing until their grunts were almost on top of us.

Miguel dug deep inside his pouch. "Pedro, I have no more stones!"

My stomach twisted and my head swam in circles, but I reached down into the water searching for stones buried in the mud. I felt only plant roots webbed around my feet.

The first Yamasee came within reach. Miguel sloshed awkwardly out of reach. Then I wrapped my fingers around a chunk of coquina the size of my hand and pulled it free from the roots. Miguel pulled it from my hand and lobbed it at the Yamasee. It hit his face. Blood gushed from his nose. Then Miguel pulled a stone from the mud and loaded his slingshot. He sent it flying before the Yamasee could act. The Indian dropped to his knees before falling backwards.

Stumbling backward with dizziness, I dropped down in water up to my chest. The English scout appeared from the other side of the cattails and caught me by the arms. I kicked wildly back and forth but he pulled me across the mud. A feeling of nausea came over me.

Miguel lunged at two Yamasees with his quarter-pike, but while he parried with one, the other attacked him from behind.

They held Miguel's legs together, pinned his arms to his side and lifted him above the water for easier transport.

My heart beat with such fervor I could feel nothing but the pounding in my chest and my lungs gasping for air. I tried to yell but my captor jammed his knee into my stomach. I heaved. My stomach emptied itself.

Then the sound of a musket fired behind us. The scout looked around and saw members of the garrison running toward us. He released his grip and took off running toward the woods. I fell into the water. The two Yamasees dropped Miguel and ran away.

Dripping from head to toe, I stumbled to my feet and pulled Grandmamma's pouch from the water. Miguel fished his quarter-pike out of the mud. The garrison ran past us and followed the enemy into the woods.

Margarita's voice called to us from the middle of the marsh. "Pedro! Miguel! Are you hurt?" She held a machete in one hand and a basket full of marsh grass in the other as she made her way toward us. "We came out to cut food for the cattle when we heard the trouble. The garrison saw the enemy from the gun deck and alerted the soldiers accompanying us."

I sat down in the mud, trying to steady the ground underneath me and looked up at the heavens, thankful for watchful eyes on the gun deck. When we were safely back inside the fort, I punched Miguel hard in the gut for his devilry with the horses and he punched me hard in the arm for my clumsiness. Despite our mishaps, it had been a good day.

18

Coquina Walls

*One may know how to conquer
without being able to do it.*— Sun Tzu

I LAY IN THE OFFICERS' QUARTERS close to Grandpapa, no longer feeling like a trapped animal in a cage but a small child under protection. Sixteen-inch-thick coquina walls and cannons capable of sinking a warship eased my trepidation after our encounter with the enemy. Even the constant chatter of the crowd no longer vexed me.

Sitting beside our straw mattress, Grandmamma pushed a cup of willow bark tea into Grandpapa's hands. He pushed it back.

"I do not need your pain reliever," he said grumpily. "Others have more need."

"Diego, you will not be less of a man by drinking my tea," she said pleadingly. She tried unsuccessfully to open his clenched fist to place the cup inside.

"My pains remind me of what has occurred," he barked. "We are at war, Leena, and my pains tell me that my actions have consequences. I will not deny my mistakes."

Grandmamma sighed, placed her tea reluctantly to the side, and pulled at the poultice covering the cut on his cheek. "Be still then. I will clean your wounds."

He swatted at her hands.

She caught his hands and held them tight. "Diego, do not fuss in front of Pedro. You are setting a bad example. He will think all men cower at the sight of a few herbs. This will not sting. Now sit still."

He looked at me, muttering under his breath. Everyone knew that when Grandmamma Leena set her mind on something, no one could change it. She placed a thin layer of animal fat on his burns before lovingly dabbing at his wounds with her ointments and special mixture of herbs. When she had finished, she stroked his hair until he fell asleep.

Then she turned her healing eyes on me. Rolling me onto my side, she poked and prodded every inch of my body. "You could have broken your neck, Pedro. The bruise on your back, where you landed on your father's bow, is severe," she said. She smoothed away a lump in the mattress before retuning me to a more comfortable position. "Remember when you were little, and you climbed a tree to look inside a mockingbird's nest? The mother bird attacked and you fell into a pile of rocks. You limped home sore and bloody. This bruise is the same. It will be sore for some time, but there are no broken bones."

"Yes, I remember that mockingbird. I could not cut wood, attend to the garden, or hunt for days because of the pain. I have learned my lesson, as I learned never to look in a mockingbird's nest again."

"Then you have grown from the experience," she said. Smoothing my hair before she left my side, she returned to watch over Grandpapa.

I waited anxiously for Miguel to return. The governor had summoned him. He alone delivered the letter we had taken from the Nombre de Dios mission. Within minutes, news spread across the courtyard telling how Zúñiga called for a meeting with his council and was not to be disturbed. I admit to feeling some jealousy toward my friend. He had an audience with the most important man in La Florida and I lay bruised in my bed.

All of a sudden, a cannon blast tore through the air. A second blast followed. Cries of fear sprang from the crowded courtyard.

Grandpapa shot up from his sleep, grabbing for a weapon that did not exist. His startled eyes combed the empty officers' quarters. "Pedro, hurry. Go up to the gun deck and see how badly the enemy has damaged the fort. They cannot breach our walls or all will be lost. Leena, help me dress. I must aid the men."

"We will wait until they call you, Diego. You must heal first," replied Grandmamma firmly.

Not waiting to hear Grandpapa's response, I ran from the room and up the ramp to the gun deck. The garrison fired on the ships in the harbor. The area smelled of burnt gunpowder. The San Agustin cannon fired a sixteen-pound cannonball, the thundering crack deafening every ear around it. I approached the southeastern wall where the blast filled my mouth, nostrils and eyes with stinging gunpowder. I spit the foul taste from my mouth.

Members of the garrison hung over the side, looking at the outside wall of the Castillo. They pointed to where the English cannonball had hit the stone. I edged closer, trying to make out what they saw.

Hysterical cattle, horses, and pigs panicked in the moat below. The soldiers talked rapidly amongst themselves.

I leaned over the wall next to them. "I am Grandpapa's eyes. Is the wall breached?"

"No, the wall holds," said Sergeant Juan Felipe. "Look."

He pointed to a place in the stone where the cannonball had landed. Instead of cracking the wall and causing it to crumble, I saw with my own eyes how the grapefruit-size ball lay buried inside the coquina brick.

"Our coquina has proven to be an unusual stone," he said. "It is porous and has allowed the cannonball to be absorbed instead of shattering the wall into pieces as intended. The English are only able to decorate our walls with their cannonballs, not bring them down."

"Their twelve-pound cannons are ineffective," said another soldier. "Tell your grandpapa Diego that our Castillo walls can withstand their attack."

Juan Felipe looked at me. "The damage may be greater if they use a heavier gun such as a sixteen-pound cannon or mortar."

I drew in a deep breath. "A mortar's arched bombs will rain shrapnel down on the people inside the courtyard. The damage would be catastrophic. The enemy must not be allowed to acquire any," I said.

Juan squeezed my shoulder. "As of now, tell your grandpapa we have seen only smaller cannons from the enemy and no mortars as of yet."

Miguel was waiting for me by the time I returned to the officers' quarters. Upon hearing my report, Grandpapa smiled for the first time since the city's siege. He lay back slowly against his straw mattress and patted Miguel on the arm. "The enemy has been halted for now. Pedro tells me you read English. Now tell us what the letter said. It may be a deception."

"But the messenger did not know we would steal the letter. How could it be a deception?" asked Miguel.

"In war, you need to know what the enemy intends to do or you cannot stop it. All through history, the communication between enemy camps has been an important source of information. The enemy realizes this. They know we will try to intercept their messages. They may send out many messengers, some of them diversions, used as bait, to lure soldiers away from the true messengers."

Miguel and I looked at each. Had we risked our lives for a lie?

"Our very own messengers carry two letters." Grandpapa leaned on his elbow, his eyes studying our expressions. "The short version is very difficult to understand. The longer version is false. The purpose of the longer version is to instill terror in the enemy. The messenger himself delivers the information orally."

"You mean the messenger might have kept everything in his head?" I asked. "And we do not possess the real message?"

"We do not know what method the English use. But we must always consider the truthfulness of anything we hear or read. It is easy to plant false rumors. Deception is a large part of war. Now tell us, Miguel, what did it say?"

Miguel looked away, translating the message in his head. "The Dios commander reports that they need iron shovels to build trenches. They want to use tools from the enemy ship *Susan* but the authorities aboard the ship will not loan them."

Grandpapa put his hand up to stop Miguel. "The enemy needs to dig trenches so they can come closer and move beyond the protection of the glacis and moat. Without shovels, the enemy cannot do this."

"That means the Nombre de Dios mission is not currently a threat," I surmised, "because the English argue amongst themselves."

Grandpapa nodded. "For now. But other locations will continue to dig trenches and threaten the fort with everything at their disposal."

Miguel continued. "They complain the machetes they were given to cut through the ground cover is dull. They suspect we are keeping cattle in the moat, because they see groups of people going out to the marsh to cut grass. They request a field glass to see better."

I smiled. "Ha! They cannot see us clearly. That is good news."

"But this news is not so good," added Miguel. "They want to sail closer so they can catch the townspeople cutting grass for the cattle, but they cannot use the creek to travel because the creek is too narrow and crooked and their canoe leaks."

"I pray they do not find another canoe," I said. "There are many hidden in the woods and along the river banks. I will sink every one of them with my axe when the opportunity arises."

"Did they speak of an attack?" asked Grandpapa.

Miguel grimaced. "*Sí, señor.* The English commander requests mortars and ammunition. He reports the soldiers' ammunition bags are empty."

"Do you think this information to be false?" Miguel asked.

"It does not appear to be false," said Grandpapa. "Only time will reveal the truth."

19

Spies Among Us

Knowledge of the enemy's dispositions can
only be obtained from other men. — Sun Tzu

THE DAYS PASSED. Fort cannons and muskets fired on the surrounding neighborhoods. A newly constructed palisade protected the fort gate from enemy gunfire. A thick blanket of gun smoke settled into the courtyard from the gun deck above.

I batted at the smoke surrounding my head, coughing. "Grandpapa says enemy trenches grow close. Our soldiers take aim, but we cannot prevent them from advancing."

Miguel waved a palm frond, trying to clear the air. "Many are in the chapel petitioning the Almighty to protect us in our time of need, day and night. My own mother prays in the chapel now."

"As does mine." I searched the crowd. "Is the pirate Andrew Ranson in the chapel still?"

"He prays, as do the others. My little brother and sister follow him everywhere. It keeps their minds off the siege and the absence of our father. The pirate has two little shadows and does not know it."

"He cannot go far unless the gates open. And they open tonight. The governor is sending a sally of soldiers this very night to burn down the houses that block our firing path to the enemy. The bow I have made from a branch here in the Castillo is inferior and will not last long. I must run like the wind before the garrison and retrieve my old bow from inside my house before they set it ablaze." Knowing what my next words would be, Miguel placed his hand on my shoulder.

I looked down. "It wounds me deeply that I have lost my father's bow. It reminded me of him."

Miguel lowered his voice. "His bow has served you well, Pedro, and this is the way of war, is it not? He would remind you of that if he were here. Be thankful that your life was spared. Did your uncle agree that you could retrieve your bow?"

I smirked at that last comment. "My uncle cannot say no if I do not seek permission."

Miguel shook his head, smiling. "You tempt fate, my friend."

We looked up in time to see Ranson depart through the chapel door and walk along the wall's inside perimeter. We followed his movements throughout the fort. He kept mostly to himself until late in the afternoon when the sun sat above the horizon. It was then that I observed him conversing with the other released prisoners.

Ranson placed an allotment of food inside his pouch and slid a pistol inside his belt. He turned to survey the movement of the soldiers after slipping a dagger inside his shoe. His eyes combed the crowd while he casually stopped to study each door and store room.

"What do you think the pirate means to do?" asked Miguel.

I was considering my reply when cousin Nico arrived. "Hey there, little cousin! You spy on our newly released prisoners? As freed men, they have the right to privacy and protection by our laws. Have you become so bored with the little games you play here in the courtyard that you turn your attention to watching our pirate?"

The smirk that covered his face annoyed me like no other. It was not easy, but I held my tongue. Grandpapa says a man must be judged by his actions and the deeds that follow, more so than the words he speaks. At least I will be able to report "I tried" if Nico pushes me further.

Nico clapped his hands, summoning the attention of the crowd. "My cousin, little Pedro, has made friends with a city boy. If the enemy breaches our walls, his city friend can demonstrate the use of fine china and how to sip from the finest goblets. We will stop the battle so our newcomer can teach the English how to be civilized!"

Nico danced in front of the crowd, lifting his legs high in the air pretending to be a dandy. Spittle flew from his face when he mimicked drinking tea from a cup with his little finger held straight in the air. The people laughed.

The hair on the back of my neck rose. "You make up falsehoods to embarrass me and my friend! You are jealous, Nico, because you have no friends! Your tongue hisses like a snake and your words are empty. Your fight is with me, not him."

The laughing stopped. A sea of eyes watched.

Nico stared, the edges of his nostrils flaring. He turned and addressed the freed prisoners. "How does my friend Andrew Ranson fair today?" he shouted.

The pirate studied Nico's face before answering. A glint shone in his eyes. "Today is a good day, *amigo*. Any day that I am not confined is a day to be praised."

Nico glanced at me before looking back at Ranson. "Beware, my friend! There are many eyes watching, including those of my little cousin and his city friend."

Ranson looked past Nico to Miguel and me. I straightened my back. Miguel crossed his arms next to me. The pirate stared with great interest. I could not and did not drop my gaze.

Ranson laughed. "Thank you for your warning, *amigo*." He waved his hand dismissively. "This citizen does not concern himself with the childish game of two young boys. They seek only to amuse themselves in times of confinement and who amongst us, beside myself, is able to provide such entertainment? I am famous, am I not?"

The crowd laughed. Ranson gave a low, sweeping bow. "Why, I am the most famous cabinetmaker in all of La Florida! Perhaps they seek to purchase one of my fine cabinets. Who can blame them?"

I felt the heat of my cheeks' rise, but others noticed only my laughter. Managing to nod approvingly against my will, I appeared to be amused to a multitude of watching eyes. When the laughter ceased, the pirate soon lost interest and turned away. Nico retreated, but not before punching me hard in the back. Reminding myself of Grandpapa's words, I held my clenched fists by my side.

Miguel let out a slow, deep breath. "Now the pirate knows."

✳✳✳

AT DUSK, we joined the garrison and townspeople crowding the gate. Everyone had come to watch the men with torches. Moving as a group, the soldiers would storm out of the fort, set fire to the surrounding neighborhoods, and return before the enemy had time to react.

It was not long before the large La Florida sun sank below the horizon and the gate opened. Waiting for an opportunity to leave unnoticed, I searched the Castillo for Nico. He was not to be found. That is when my eyes fell on someone moving along the northeast side of the gun deck. The figure suddenly disappeared over the wall. My heart jumped inside my chest.

Turning toward the open gate and following the men carrying torches, I pushed Miguel through the crowd and out of the Castillo. "Hurry! We follow the pirate, Andrew Ranson!"

20

Deceit and Trickery

Though the enemy be stronger in numbers, we may prevent him from fighting. Scheme so as to discover his plans and the likelihood of their success. — Sun Tzu

THE PIRATE ANDREW RANSON had taken advantage of the distraction to escape the fort. Only Miguel and I knew of his cunning.

After crossing the marsh, we dodged a thicket of biting palmetto blades before stopping to listen to the sounds of the woods. To listen carefully means life or death in the wild.

Eyes closed, I could hear my labored breaths, the pounding beat of blood rushing through my ears, and then a very faint crackling of branches and dry leaves in the distance. Opening my eyes to the dark, I pointed in the direction of the noise, praying it was not a group of armadillos searching for water. I was certain, however, that the pirate Andrew Ranson traveled unaware of our presence. We moved forward.

A full moon glowed against the night sky, offering us ample light. That also meant Ranson moved with the same advantage. An owl hooted overhead; tree frogs croaked as a thin mist of rain fell. Rustling noises sounded in many directions.

I stopped. "Ranson is not moving," I whispered. "I cannot tell which direction he takes."

Miguel looked ahead. "Where would a prisoner go?"

"This I do know. He does not walk toward the mission where the soldiers stay. He walks west toward the river."

"Perhaps he looks for a canoe."

I turned, searching in all directions. Had I taken the wrong path? Or followed a group of deer now grazing on berries and bushes?

Miguel pointed in the distance. A faint glow emerged above

the ground. "Someone builds a fire."

I studied the location. "To light a fire in the middle of enemy territory means this person has confidence in his safety, something our pirate does not have."

"If it is the enemy, we must alert the garrison."

"What would we tell them, Miguel? That the enemy warms themselves with a fire in the middle of the woods? The enemy is everywhere. They have taken the city, they have taken our missions, and their ships wait outside our harbor. Enemy in the woods is no different than enemy elsewhere. They command the land."

"Yes, but this enemy is not under cannon or army protection."

I nodded in thought. "Your words are wise, Miguel. We will go see who warms themselves by the fire."

Miguel hesitated. "Should we not warn the garrison first? This is a matter for soldiers with muskets and pikes. And what of the pirate?"

I gripped the top of my axe. "I have my bow and axe, and you have your slingshot and quarter-pike. The pirate cannot know the area. He will distance himself from the Castillo but will wait for dawn to continue. He will not risk capture by Indians or fortune hunters."

This calmed Miguel's fear and we moved quietly and slowly toward the campfire where a thick wall of shrub protected us from view. The fire crackled, spitting flames high into the air. Two men walked on the outside of the fire, clearing the ground of leaves and mounds of pine needles around it, keeping the flames from spreading to the dry ground cover. The air around us grew warmer the nearer we came.

Three enemy soldiers and two Indians warmed their hands by the fire. One roasted fish on a long stick. They were deep in conversation until one of the Indians said something to make them all laugh. I waited anxiously for Miguel to translate.

His eyebrows pinched together as he strained to hear. "The Indians are going to the fort tomorrow and will beg to be brought inside. They will say they are not safe, that Indians loyal to England have slaughtered other members of their tribe and they seek God's mercy inside the fort where the Spanish will keep them from harm.

They will offer false news of where the English are camped and the movements of the troops."

I shook my head. "This news will be dear to the governor. I fear if we do not interfere, the garrison will allow them to enter."

Miguel held his finger to his lips, listening. "Once they are inside, they will turn the other Indians against the Spanish. They will promise them many treasures and great honor. They will tell them the English are great in numbers and powerful; the English will win an easy victory and the Indians must be with the victors or perish with the others when they storm the Castillo. Once the spies have earned the loyalty of the Indians inside the fort, they will plot to kill the officers and overtake the Castillo."

I squeezed the handle of my axe. "The garrison must be warned of this treachery. But we must also stop the pirate. He too, has the power to bring down the Castillo. If we go back to the Castillo and warn the garrison, they will catch the spies but the pirate will take flight. If we follow the pirate, and the Indians enter the Castillo, they will turn the other Indians."

"Then we must go our separate ways," Miguel said. "I will warn the garrison in the Castillo and you follow the pirate."

"That is too dangerous, Miguel. We are under a blanket of darkness and you do not fully understand the ways of the woods. No, we must listen to all that they say, wait till they go to sleep, then go in search of the pirate in the morning. As soon as we are able, we must return to the Castillo. I take comfort in knowing it will take some time for the spies to turn the others against us. Pray that we return in time."

Feeling anxious, but confident in our decision, we waited for the men to sleep, but they entertained themselves by laughing and playing cards. We had no choice but to settle on the ground and wait. Something I did not expect was the warmth of the fire bathing us in such soothing heat that my eyelids grew heavy. If not for the actions of another soldier bursting into camp, I would have fallen asleep. His job as lookout had been unknown to us. How his existence escaped my detection concerned me, but I did not have time to dwell upon it.

Shaking his head awake, Miguel quickly translated the newcomer's words. "Cover the fire . . . a Spanish patrol passes . . . they will see the fire and we will be discovered!"

I sat up, suddenly fully alert. Studying our surroundings, I searched the trees under the glow of firelight. A group of towering pine trees grew in the distance. Brush and thickets of ground cover filled the area, but a small path led under the trees where the surface was bare. "Hurry, we must look for green pinecones not yet open. They will be hard to distinguish in the dark, so gather all that are closed. We must pray that we have chosen wisely."

Thankfully, Miguel did not question my motive and moved with haste. We crawled on hands and knees through walls of shrub until reaching flat ground full of pine needles. Miguel patted the area under the trees and I searched the mounds of pine needles scattered throughout the surface. Pinecones were plentiful and it took only moments to find what we needed.

Back at the camp, the men kicked sand and dirt into the fire, only it did not impede the flames. Heavy with pine needle and dried leaves, the fire continued to burn. We moved unnoticed back into the area.

"How many pinecones have you gathered?" I asked.

"Maybe ten."

"I count the same. It is the green pinecones that hold pine oil inside; the others will be useless. If we have not gathered the cones we need, or the fire is not hot enough, we will fall into enemy hands. Are you ready?"

My words gave Miguel pause, but he nodded as expected.

"Do not run until you see my signal."

Crawling behind the thicket closest to the fire, I pulled the top layer of my tunic off and placed the bundle of pinecones inside. After folding it to appear as wadded clothing, I hoped to drop the bundle into the fire. If all went as planned, the soldiers would worry more about me than a bundle of burning cloth.

Tucking the bundle under my arm, I squatted in position, studying the path before me. I drew in a deep breath before turning toward my friend. He nodded.

The enemy had their backs to us. A small fire continued to burn even though they labored to smother it. When they bent down to gather more dirt, I sprinted out of my hiding place and keeping my eyes on the fire, dropped the bundle inside. Surprised at my sudden appearance, two of the soldiers abandoned their task and took chase after me. Then something happened that I did not take into account. The bright image of the firelight blinded the path before me and I fell face down in the dirt.

A pair of hands pulled me up. "Hold on to me, Pedro. Run! They mean to kill us!"

21

Trapped

Though we have heard of stupid haste in war, cleverness has never been seen associated with long delays. — Sun Tzu

MIGUEL STEERED US DOWN the escape path I had shared earlier. I stumbled clumsily over tree roots and branches blocking our path, but he held me tight by the belt and did not let go. Fortunately, the blinding images faded and my sight returned.

The two soldiers from the campfire crashed through the thicket behind us. I broke free of Miguel's grip and ran into a towering sawgrass thicket straight ahead. The small spines covering the surface of the long thin leaves tore my trousers and tunic into pieces. Blood ran down my legs. The outer layer of my right trouser leg hung in shreds. Gasping for breath, I turned to face the enemy while reaching for my bow.

The men hesitated at the outside edge of the thicket, allowing me enough time to pull an arrow from my quiver and fix it in place. The first man rushed into the sawgrass after me. The familiar swoosh of Miguel's slingshot tore past my ears. I drew the bow back and let go. The arrow landed in the man's chest close to his shoulder. Blood soaked his uniform, but he continued to charge.

I tore the axe from my belt ready to fight, but Miguel's slingshot found its mark first. The soldier fell backwards into the thicket and disappeared from sight. I placed another arrow in my bow and aimed it at the soldier behind him. The second man charged the thicket of sawgrass but was hindered by the thick growth of blades. His ripped uniform hung in pieces.

Before I could take aim, a loud bang rang out in the distance. Then another. And another. The green pinecones I had thrown into the heat burst with such force that the explosion reverberated through the woods like gunshots. The second soldier broke free of the thicket and fled. Pointing the tip of my arrow at his silhouette as he passed the trees, I released the arrow but he veered left and the arrow lodged inside a tree.

Using my bow to part the leaves in front of me, I moved slowly out of the thicket into the path. Strips of cloth hung on the spines where our bodies had passed. My own leg stung from where the spines had ripped the skin open.

Miguel grinned. "We won, Pedro!"

I rubbed the gashes covering my right leg. "Do not pat yourself on the back, my friend. If given the chance, the enemy will return with the others. Come, let us see if the garrison approaches the campsite because of the noise."

We moved quietly toward the campsite. The art of doing the unexpected during battle was a matter for discussion later. Miguel had survived our encounter uninjured. His trousers remained intact and his skin free of scratches because he had kept to the open path where all could reach him. When the enemy chose to attack me first, it was chance that spared him, not skill or strategy. I knew the impact of my words pointing out the foolishness of this move would fall short after our victory, but it was a necessary conversation for later.

Musket fire rang out. Shouting followed. I pulled Miguel behind the bushes where we crept cautiously along the side toward the campsite. It wasn't until we heard our native language did we emerge. The English soldiers and two Indians lay prone on the ground. Three members of the garrison secured their hands with rope.

Realizing the danger had passed, I stepped boldly from the bushes. "Good evening, Sergeant." I pointed behind me. "Another soldier lies injured inside the thicket of sawgrass just beyond those pine trees. An arrow adorns his shoulder and there is a knot on his head from my friend's slingshot. We have learned that the enemy plots to infiltrate the Castillo. The Indians work as spies and intend to enter the Castillo in order to turn Indians loyal to Spain against us."

The sergeant frowned at first, but offered a small smile when he had taken stock of the enemy. "How is it that you have signaled me, Pedro? Are you not confined to the Castillo? It has been several months since hearing your pinecones burst like gunfire. Very clever, using one of your hunting tricks on the enemy. I recall you flushing a large buck out into the open last time, no?"

"You remember well, Sergeant. The hide of that buck made this fine pouch and the buckskin trousers I wear today. A thicket of sawgrass desired to tear the flesh from my body, but my buckskin trousers have kept me from serious harm."

The *capitán* pointed to where the buckskin had torn open on my right leg and gashes covered the bloody skin. "It appears, young Pedro, that your buck has had its revenge."

The soldiers laughed. The enemy twisted their heads around trying to see.

I nodded. "I am thankful that I still have the use of my legs and my life."

The Sargent folded his arms. "Does your uncle send you into enemy territory?"

"No, Sergeant. I only seek to help the Crown, not worry my uncle and my grandpapa."

"I suspect it is your mother and your grandmamma who worry. Your grandfather has faith in you, as does your uncle, although he cannot say this aloud. You have not told me why you are here, Pedro."

My hesitation did not go unnoticed. I could not tell him of the pirate Andrew Ranson, because he would make me return to the Castillo, and the pirate was under my charge. My uncle and Grandpapa had placed the burden of watching the pirate on me. Perhaps they did so to keep my thoughts occupied, or perhaps they did so because I alone had time to observe such things. I will not burden the garrison with a matter I could handle on my own. They now faced the added danger of getting the English prisoners past the enemy and into the Castillo because of me, so I felt no shame in my answer. "I came to gather herbs for Grandmamma and find wood for a new bow. Enemy trenches grow near."

The Sargent frowned. "That they do. If the enemy breaches the walls, you will need your bow and many arrows. I cannot deny you this." He pointed to Miguel. "I hear your new friend is the perfect companion. He does not shy away from your folly."

The soldiers laughed once again.

Miguel stepped forward. "I am happy to have a friend such as Pedro. He has been teaching me the ways of the New World. And the ways of battle."

"And yet you are not covered in blood and our Pedro is." He chuckled before placing his hand on my shoulder. "I know Pedro to be a good teacher. His father was a good friend and his son follows in his footsteps. Your father, Miguel, remains in Apalachee where I have just departed. They guard the mission from the uprising and keep the local Indian tribes content. He fulfills his duty by keeping the war from spreading. I will not tell him of your journey outside the Castillo and into enemy territory. Your safety in this matter does not need to worry him further."

Miguel looked down. "Thank you, Sergeant. Pedro and I are skilled at taking care of ourselves. If he were here, he would know of this."

"Of this, I have no doubt. Pedro knows every inch of woods and the ways of survival. No animal is safe if he decides to hunt. Because of this, I will not escort you back to the Castillo, but you must use caution. The enemy fills the woods. At the moment, the garrison is able to send messengers across the land, but at great risk. The enemy plots to cut us off at every opportunity, and your journey back to the Castillo will be perilous. You can only return by way of the marsh."

I slid my bow into place and secured my axe. "This I understand, Sergeant. Tell my mother and Grandmamma not to worry. I will bring fresh herbs and a bow able to withstand the English. And if I am able, Sergeant, I will bring you back some persimmons."

Smiling, the sergeant squeezed my shoulder. "Ah, young Pedro remembers my fondness for persimmon pudding. Go with God's speed, boys. We will talk again inside the Castillo."

Then he turned toward his men as they prepared to travel with the prisoners. We bid the garrison farewell and hurried toward the riverbank knowing that the sergeant might rethink his position and change his mind at any moment.

22

Tracking the Pirate

Bring war material with you from home, but forage on the enemy.
Thus the army will have food enough for its needs. — Sun Tzu

GLIMPSES OF A FULL MOON shone through the tree cover. Bats circled overhead in the night sky. Miguel and I stepped carefully through the underbrush searching for the pirate. Ground heavy with scrub blocked our path.

The river stood ahead. "We will find shelter for the night and look for the pirate when the sun begins to rise above the sea again."

Anxiety filled Miguel's voice. "Pedro, we did not prepare for the night. We have no food, only the water in our canteen, and no coverings for sleep during the frozen night."

His words echoed my own concern. "Many of the natives had to flee into the Castillo when the English army came. I search for an abandoned home that does not stand with the others. Pray the enemy has not taken residence inside."

We walked in silence some distance until reaching a clearing at the river's edge, where the remains of a burned-out village stood. Huts, once sturdy and strong, lay ruined in ashes. The wild had begun to reclaim the land, the overgrown gardens now filled with encroaching plants.

The members of this tribe had been my friends. They had warmed me by the winter fire, filled my ears with stories, filled my stomach with food, and traded my pelts for pottery. My grandmamma had grown up among them. Many were family.

My throat grew tight as I struggled to speak. "It is as I feared. The enemy has destroyed the homes so none may take shelter."

Forced to push my memories aside, we moved farther up the riverbank looking for a place to sleep. Large rocks lining the bank slowed our pace, but our speed improved once we reached level ground. Alligators live in fresh water, and wild animals come to drink along the water's edge at night, making this very spot a busy watering hole. Not wanting to encounter the dangers that waited, I led us away into the woods.

A large distance had passed before reaching a thicket of sawgrass where a single hut stood. Faint images of overgrown plants blocked a clear entrance to the hut. Squatting on bended knee, we crawled through the small opening to a floor covered in deerskins. The remains of broken pottery shards lay scattered from one side of the hut to the other. Either the occupant had left in a hurry or animals had knocked the clay pots over seeking food.

Setting my bow to the side, I readied for sleep. "It is dark and because of this, we are safe here tonight. The deerskins will keep us warm, and the walls will keep the cold winds off our backs. At dawn, we will feast on nuts and ripe fruit while tracking the pirate."

The deerskins offered sufficient warmth once we rolled them into cocoons and crawled inside. Miguel pulled his quarter-pike close to his body before falling asleep. For me, sleep did not come so easily. I listened for the enemy and the many signs of danger in the wild at night. Trials to come worried me more than passing panthers and black bears.

Morning eventually vanquished the night. Miguel awoke with a yawn. I gathered my things and moved into the open woods, with Miguel trailing closely behind. A strong scent of pine hung in the air. My empty stomach growled. My friend's stomach signaled hunger, too, but he kept it to himself. A large clay urn, used to catch rainwater, stood close to the hut entrance. We drank until our stomachs were full and replenished the water inside our wooden canteens.

Continuing our search for the pirate, we struggled through dense ground cover looking for food. Absent were the hickory nuts, persimmons, cocoplums, pond apples, and Muscadine grapes. I hold no fondness for the bitter acorn but I would have consumed a bowlful to quiet my empty stomach. "The enemy scours the woods and eats everything it finds," I sighed.

Miguel said nothing but his pursed lips told me of his hunger. We continued to push through the brush when I spotted a sweetgum tree in the distance, its sap hardened on the trunk.

Upon our arrival, I pried two chunks of sap off the trunk and offered one to Miguel. "Chew this but do not swallow. It will keep your hunger down and your jaws busy."

Miguel did as I bid, but not without reservation. He tasted it first before placing it inside his mouth. He was reluctant to chew it at first, but once the mildly bitter sap softened, he nodded with approval.

I removed two more chunks of sap and placed them inside my pouch for later. "The body can live many days without food, but it cannot live without water. We will drink often and fill our canteens with clean rainwater when we come upon it. As long as we have water, we will remain strong."

Pedro looked away. "I pray that we find food farther inside the woods. My stomach does not want to test your words. Where do we go now, Pedro?"

"We walk toward the ocean. The pirate consumed my thoughts last night when my mind would not rest. A pirate makes his living on the water. He knows this well. If he seeks to escape, he will look for a boat."

Swamp water soaked our shoes and sharp palmetto leaves tore at our legs, but we pushed ahead toward the rising sun. Evidence of the enemy's hunt for food continued to appear as we passed scraps of animal remains along the ground. Despite our trial, we welcomed the fresh, cold breeze blowing through the trees. Then I spotted something in the distance and led us through a long patch of cypress knees to a group of swamp cabbage plants.

Taking my axe from my belt, I cut the swamp cabbage where the stalk bends up from the ground and leaves sprout from the top. Using the blade like a knife, I cut away the tough outside until the white, tender center of the palm plant lay in my hand. I sliced it into rounds and gave a handful to Miguel. There was enough of the white fleshy meat to fill our stomachs and add to our pouches for later.

With our appetites temporarily satisfied, we continued on our journey, halting only long enough to gather herbs before stopping at the bottom of an old magnolia tree.

"We must climb to the top," I said. "It is a challenging task. You can climb a tree, can you not?"

He snorted. "Want to bet on it?"

I laughed. "No. I have to come trust your skills. Make it to the top and I will let you teach me the ways of a slingshot."

He smirked.

The tallest tree in the forest, the old magnolia's hundred-foot trunk grew straight up past the others. It was tiring, backbreaking work to climb to the top. After an hour of stopping and starting, gasping for breath, and pushing our muscles until they ached, we broke above the tree line to admire a breathtaking view below. In the distance, enemy ships sat motionless at sea. South of us, smoke from the Castillo's gun deck rose as the cannons fired unsuccessfully across the sandbar.

Shielding my eyes from the glaring sun, I studied the beach bordering the woods where we sat. "Now we watch for the pirate and witness the deeds of the enemy."

23

The Enemy

Thus, what is of supreme importance in war is to attack the enemy's strategy. — Sun Tzu

MIGUEL AND I SAW NINE MEN and a stack of six trunks standing next to three longboats beached on the dunes. Two negroes, three native Indians, and a white man sat tied together on the sand. The mast of a nearby brigantine rose above the sandbar horizon.

I looked toward the Castillo, wondering how far the distance and how many of the enemy blocked the path. As I feared, the inland position of the beach hid the ship from the garrison's view. "Those poor souls will be sold as slaves."

Miguel studied the brigantine. "What can we do?"

"And those trunks are made locally. I will bet my next meal that they hold the town's stolen valuables. Perhaps the enemy moves its booty to a different location for safekeeping."

"Perhaps," Miguel said. "But why risk capture so close to the Castillo? If those trunks contain treasure, I bet my next meal that the enemy trades for something of great importance on that ship."

I stared at the men struggling to break free of their bindings. "There may be some truth to your words, Miguel. We need to know what those trunks carry and what it is they purchase."

Miguel squinted into the sun. "How, my friend? We are not able to call the garrison and by the time we get back to the Castillo, the ship will have sailed."

"Then we must get closer to the enemy and learn what we can."

It was then that I descended the long path down the tree trunk to the ground, thinking only of prisoners, what booty filled the trunks, and the danger ahead. Informing Miguel of my intent had not occurred to me, nor did I turn to see if he followed. In my haste, I neglected to survey the woods for the enemy. Only a jolter-head would make such a mistake. Acting as if I did not have a care in the world, I dropped down in front of two enemy soldiers as they cleared a wall of palmettos on their way to the beach.

Of course, they saw me long before I saw them. Before I could assess my surroundings, a bayonet pushed against my cheek. Two ill-tempered soldiers relieved me of my bow, my axe, my knife, my pouch, and my canteen before tying my hands behind my back and binding my ankles loosely with rope.

The anger I felt for being such a fool gripped my heart like a clenched fist. I wanted to scream. I wanted to kick. I wanted to bite anyone within reach. It took everything I had to look at the ground instead of glancing toward the tree for signs of Miguel.

24

Prisoner of War

In battle, there are not more than two methods of attack — the direct and the indirect; yet these two in combination give rise to an endless series of maneuvers. — Sun Tzu

THE ANGER CONSUMING my insides punched me hard in the gut like a fist. Once again Grandpapa and the garrison had been correct in their assessment of boys fighting in war. We do not have the experience, the wisdom, or discipline to be effective soldiers. Muttering under my breath, I chastised myself for being stupid.

The soldiers frog-marched me to the edge of the woods where the tree line meets the beach and the other prisoners waited. They expertly hid my bow, axe, and knife inside a thicket of saw palmetto before drinking the water from my canteen and eating the heart of palm from inside my pouch. When they tried the herbs I had gathered for Grandmamma, they made a face and spit the remains into the air. If I had not been so angry at myself, I would have laughed. Grandmamma used those herbs to treat seeping wounds. The acidic leaves blister the tongue.

We stepped onto the beach, the frigid ocean air sending shivers down my back. Directly in front of us, two longboats rode back across the choppy waters toward the brigantine. One of the trunks and a prisoner remained behind on the beach. The others bobbed inside the longboats as they steered toward the ship.

The soldiers pushed me against the other prisoner, tied our hands behind our backs and faced us in the opposite direction. I faced the woods. Thankfully, I would be able to see Miguel if he were there. I craned my neck, trying to see the face of the other prisoner, but my view was limited to the corners of my eyes. The prisoner spoke in English to the soldiers but they scoffed and walked away. He turned toward me, but I could not see enough of his face to recognize him.

He laughed. "They desire to watch the longboats as the soldiers deliver their prisoners to the *capitán,* instead of chat with me. They are ignorant louts but malleable. Give me time, and I will turn their heads. So, how is it that Pedro finds himself on this side of the Castillo walls?"

I twisted my neck trying to see but to no avail. "Andrew Ranson. I am relieved to hear your voice. I have been tracking your escape from the Castillo."

"Is that so? Your entertainment is not limited to the Castillo, where I kept you and your little friends busy. Now you have joined me as a prisoner. Very thoughtful. I did not realize we were such good *amigos.*"

"I came to stop you from telling the English about the Castillo and the actions of the garrison."

"Is that all? It seems you are too late. I have told them much, and they treat me as royalty. Tonight, I dine on beef fillet and drink the finest wines. Tomorrow, I will be the *capitán* of that fine brigantine and lead the English to victory." Then he paused and his voice softened. "Aww, that brigantine. In truth, I cannot take my eyes off of that beauty. She is one hundred and fifty tons, eighty feet long, and carries ten cannons ready for battle. I am in love."

I did not know what to make of his words. "How is it that you are captured? I saw you head into the woods, away from here."

"Sixteen years living inside the Castillo has made me as rusty as an old cabinet's door hinge. I awoke to find those two fine gentlemen pointing their bayonets at my person. They were kind enough to lighten my load by relieving me of my knives and my food."

"But they are the English. That is who you sought to find."

"My dear boy, you have much to learn. Why would I seek out the very people who have placed a reward on my head? Some very wealthy merchants with very long memories have placed a rather sizeable bounty on my head—and I am rather fond of my head. It is a handsome head and the ladies favor it."

"If this is true, why would they not seek out your knowledge of the Castillo first, then turn you over for the reward?"

"Listen to me, boy, because this is important. You do not want to be on the losing side when the war is over. As far as they know,

I have lived inside a prison cell and know nothing. I will not help anybody that seeks to cover me in boiling tar and hang me inside an iron cage to rot. The reward on my head and prestige at bringing me back in chains speaks louder than any words, which they would not trust, in place of my freedom."

"Then why did you leave the safety of the Castillo?"

"I am a prisoner, young Pedro. I do not come and go like yourself. I am told when to wake up, what to eat, what to do, when to go to bed. I cannot play cards, join the others in celebration, or partake in Sunday dinners. I do not share my life with friends or family. And there may come a day when Spain orders my death. Would you not do the same?"

I hesitated, not having considered such things. To live such a life would have vexed me beyond hope, but I could not admit this to him. "I do not understand. If you do not seek out the English, where were you going?"

He chuckled. "I was going to see my sweetheart, Kathryn. This lovely lady waits for me in Virginia. I have prayed both day and night for nothing else. The friars have been kind enough to pass along her letters to me for many years. I plan to relieve those lads of their brigantine so I can sail her to Virginia, but the way to do this has not presented itself yet."

I frantically twisted my bindings with everything I had trying to loosen the knot, but to my angst, the knot pulled tighter. "What is your plan? What does the brigantine carry?"

"Ah, now you ask an intelligent question. I was beginning to worry about you, boy. I have gleaned from those two knotheads standing guard over us that this fine brigantine delivers a mortar and a sixteen-pound iron cannon, and for a very handsome price, too. They wait for a flood tide so they can bring the ship closer to shore and deliver the heavy artillery."

Those words twisted my stomach into a knot. The Castillo stood because the enemy did not possess the heavy guns needed to breach her walls, but a mortar and sixteen-pound cannon were such beasts. It was a cruel twist of fate to learn this news as a prisoner. "We have to get free."

Ranson roared with laughter. "Is this your plan, Little Bird?

To announce that we must get free? Feeble words from a feeble boy."

Every muscle in my body tensed. He mocked me.

"Your father was a good man and a good soldier. You are not worthy of being his son. It is good that your father, bless his soul, is not here to see his little *niño* cower. He would turn his head in shame and chastise himself for failing as a father. He turns in his grave as we speak. You are nothing but an embarrassment."

The hairs on the back of my neck bristled. If he meant to vex me, he had succeeded.

I rammed into his back, seeking to knock him over, but he moved forward to even my blow. My insides churned in fury; Ranson chuckled at my actions. Screaming at the top of my lungs, I snapped my head back with such force that the pain momentarily paralyzed my neck. My skull hit him hard between the shoulders, knocking the breath out of him.

Ranson leaned forward, shouting, "This little bird has a temper! Easy now, Little Bird, before the cats come to investigate."

It was then that the soldiers heard the commotion and came running. I dug my heels into the sand and pushed with all my might. Ranson pulled himself forward, countering my move. I screamed again. He laughed as we edged across the sand with me hitting his back with my head and him scooting forward to minimize my blows.

The soldiers ran at us with their bayonets out. Ranson cursed at them. The larger soldier punched me in the shoulder with the butt of his musket. I doubled over in pain. The other one kicked Ranson in the stomach. He crumbled. They pushed us apart and cut the rope tying us together.

The smaller soldier pulled me across the beach by the collar. Sand poured into every opening of my clothes and into the tops of my shoes. I spit the gritty white stuff from my mouth and shook the sand from my hair. He tied me to the base of a palm tree.

Both soldiers pulled Ranson toward the water. He spit at them. The larger soldier hit him in the head with his fist. Ranson fell over, but he managed a wink before they dragged him inside the last longboat. I fell back against the tree and looked up at the large blue sky, realizing the pirate had planned this all along.

25

Don't Follow My Folly

The Moral Law causes the people to be in complete accord with their ruler, so that they will follow him regardless of their lives, undismayed by any danger. — Sun Tzu

I LOOKED AROUND for anything sharp to cut my bindings, but found only small round shells buried beneath the sand. Seagulls circled overhead, their calls echoing like laughter in the air. I had only a short amount of time before the two soldiers delivered Ranson to the crew of the brigantine and came back for me.

"Psst! Pedro, move around the tree and face the ocean so I can reach your bindings. I will crawl out and cut you free."

The sound of Miguel's voice filled my heart with hope. "Wait for my signal. The soldiers watch me from the boat. One stands ready with his musket." Looking down so as not to draw attention, I inched slowly around the base of the palm tree and faced the ocean to block their view of Miguel. "Why did you not go back to the Castillo and warn the garrison? The brigantine carries heavy guns."

The longboat began to row Ranson toward the brigantine. The small soldier did not take his eyes off me. Then Ranson rose up from the bottom of the boat and started yelling.

My heart jumped. "Now, Miguel. Hurry! Ranson distracts them."

Miguel crawled quickly across the sand on his belly, and sawed at the rope binding my wrists. Ranson tried to jump over the side of the boat but the soldiers yanked him to the floor of the boat where it rocked uncontrollably in the water. Loud curses flew from Ranson's lips. The larger soldier strapped a gag around the pirate's mouth, but he thrashed wildly back and forth, almost tipping the boat. The smaller soldier hit him in the head with an oar. Ranson fell to the bottom of the boat and did not rise. A lump formed in my throat. I prayed the bounty did not say dead or alive.

My bindings broke free. I slid along the ground before disappearing into a thicket of scrub. A shot rang out behind us. The bullet hit the ground, spitting sand everywhere. Both soldiers pointed to where Miguel and I had entered the woods. The longboat turned and started back toward the shore.

I shoved Miguel ahead. "You return to the Castillo and warn them. The pirate is in need of my help."

Miguel stopped in his tracks. "Then I must remain, Pedro. If the pirate needs your help, you will need mine. Where you go, I go."

"There is no time to argue, Miguel. The Castillo must be warned and I cannot go."

Miguel shook his head. "But, Pedro, the Castillo can do nothing. We are under siege. As long as the enemy stays out of reach and out of sight of our cannons, the garrison is unable to stop them. You have said this yourself. I go with you."

Biting my lower lip to keep from screaming at him, I said nothing and moved quickly toward the palmettos where my possessions lay. When I found the exact location, I crawled under the thicket and retrieved my axe, bow, canteen, knife, and a second knife that did not belong to me.

Then I faced my stubborn friend. "Come, Miguel, we must hide in the trees before the enemy comes ashore."

The sound of crunching leaves and snapping branches echoed as we hastened through the dense shrub and woods. Gasping for breath, we stopped at the massive tree trunk we had descended earlier. Miguel jumped for the lowest branch but I pulled him down.

He bent over panting. "What is it we do, Pedro?"

I pointed toward the beach. "We left a trail that a blind man could follow and a deaf bear could hear. They will not be able to see us, but they will assume we have climbed this tree and this is where they will try to trap us. In the meantime, we will retreat back to the beach to help Ranson."

Miguel smiled for the first time this day. We backed slowly away from the tree trunk, stepping in between the ferns and scrub, careful to leave no visible footprints. Rustling noises, created by the enemy, crept toward the tree from the other side of the woods. A tall thicket of plants hid us from view as we edged our way back to the beach.

Ranson stood in the middle of the beached longboat, tied to both ends of the boat. A rosy red knot covered the side of his head. He grinned when he saw us. "I knew you'd come, boy. Your papa was right. You are a clever little bird."

Miguel lifted his knife to cut Ranson's bindings, but I pushed his hand away. "We do not free him. He must board the brigantine as a prisoner. I do not have time to explain but you must trust me on this."

Miguel looked confused but did as I bid.

"What do you need from us, Ranson?" I asked.

"Slip a knife into my shoe and loosen the bindings around my hands. Not too loose, mind you. Those two Englishmen may be simpletons but they will notice a bad knot. I saw you shimmy down that magnolia earlier. It was I who alerted the soldiers to your whereabouts. I will need your help on the ship."

Miguel pointed his knife at Ranson. "It is your fault we run for our lives? Why should we help you now?"

"Because we fight for the same side, boy. I must commandeer this fine brigantine or your troubles will grow inside the Castillo if they deliver those heavy guns. She will not survive a mortar or bigger cannon and I cannot do it alone. Now, hurry before our enemy grows weary of the chase and returns."

Miguel looked at me.

I pushed his knife away from Ranson's face. "He fights for the Spanish Crown, Miguel. He is free and our only chance of sinking the guns that can destroy the fort."

Miguel reluctantly used the tip of his quarter-pike to loosen the bindings around the pirate's wrist while I lifted the second dagger from my shoe to transfer to the pirate's shoe. It did not fit as it should.

"Hey! Careful there, Little Bird! Mind the toes. I do not fancy losing any of them today. Turn the knife's blade toward my heel where the ankle does not bend. When I reach for it, I must be able to draw it, blade out. I will not die until I see my Kathryn again or I will take every one of these stinking louts with me."

I turned the blade around as he asked.

He smiled. "Ah, that's better. Now, go look in that last trunk and tell me what she holds. The soldiers do not go near it and load it last. They fear whatever it carries."

Miguel watched the trees. "Pedro, we must go before the soldiers return."

I stared at the trunk. It was bigger and longer than the others. A latch held the lid in place but it did not hold a lock. Checking the entrance to the woods one last time, I walked over to the trunk and placed my hands on top. "Warn me if you see or hear anything. If this treasure belongs to the town, we will take it back with us. Its treasure will offer hope to the people."

Miguel started to protest but Ranson shook his head to silence him. I moved the latch and lifted the lid up. The air filled with the smell of rotten pond scum. I swatted at the air trying to clear the smell. "Phew!"

Ranson pulled at his ropes trying to see. "What is it?"

Miguel craned his neck to look inside. "It's an alligator. A dead juvenile. And it's big."

Ranson nodded in admiration. "So, that is what all the fuss was about earlier." He studied the woods before continuing. "That meat will feed a hungry crew and an alligator hide will command a fair price. One of those blokes will be separating the flesh from the skin before it rots this very day."

I looked back and forth between the beach and the woods. "Miguel, help me dump the alligator in the scrub." I tugged on the heavy trunk.

"Why? We do not have time. Let them keep their alligator."

I frowned at him. "Trust me."

Miguel stood beside me. Using our combined strength to pull the heavy load, we slid the trunk slowly across the sand. The drag marks that followed were deep. Once we reached the edge of the scrub, we rolled the trunk over. The heavy alligator made a loud, crashing thump when it hit the thicket. The thick wall of plants swallowed the body of the alligator, but the snout, with its row of sharp pointed teeth, hung out in the path. We hurried to push the massive jaws under the thicket.

Ranson yelled at us, but we could not make out his words. Rain drops began to fall from the darkening sky. I pulled the empty trunk with great speed toward the longboat while Miguel used his foot and a palm frond to smooth away the deep drag marks.

"The crows take flight from the trees," Ranson yelled. "They come, boys. Take cover!"

"Hurry, run back to the woods, Miguel. You will be safe until the longboat is gone."

"And you, Pedro?"

"Do as I say, Miguel. I help the pirate by hiding in the trunk. Do not risk your life. Go back to the Castillo and warn them. If something happens to me, tell my grandpapa that he lives in my heart always, and tell my mother, my grandmamma, and my uncle that I love them."

Miguel did not move. "I will not leave you, Pedro. We must both be in the trunk to equal the weight of the alligator. It is I who saves you."

My heart pounded inside my chest. "Do not concern yourself with this. Go, Miguel, there is no time to argue. It is urgent that the Castillo know of the heavy artillery. As my friend, it is important that you do this for me."

He stared.

"Go, Miguel, now!"

"Go now, boy, or join the fight." Ranson shouted. "Another minute and there will be no choice."

Miguel hesitated. Then he turned and ran toward the trees. Holding my bow close to me, I opened the trunk and jumped in. The inside smelled of alligator and foul swamp water but I cared not. If my plan to get safely on board did not work, I would have signed my own death warrant but spared Miguel the same folly. Just as my heart calmed and my breathing slowed to a quiet whisper, the lid opened, and Miguel, holding his quarter-pike tightly in his hand, jumped in next to me.

26

Face-to-Face with the Enemy

Now the general who wins a battle makes many
calculations in his temple ere the battle is fought. — Sun Tzu

BECAUSE I WAS BORN to a military family, I was taught the ways of war, the skills to survive, the importance of honor, the meaning of sacrifice, and the necessity of protecting others. My father learned this from his father and his father learned it before him. I do not take my life, or the lives of others around me, for granted. All life is precious, but it is the way of the world that each of us will die. When we will die is the great unknown, but for me, it is how I die that matters.

Ranson spoke first with taunts aimed at distracting the soldiers from the trunk. Thankfully, Miguel was there to translate. My task would have been harder, maybe impossible, without his knowledge of the English language. I had not realized this before.

"It took your majesties long enough," he called. "The rain comes. Am I to wait for lightning to strike? Your wealthy merchants would not pay for a corpse burnt to cinders."

There was a grunt and then a thump as the pirate hit the bottom of the longboat. Then the latch slid shut on top of the trunk, trapping Miguel and me inside. A lump grew in my throat. I squeezed my eyes shut, concentrating on the noises coming from outside.

Grunting under the weight, the two soldiers lifted the heavy trunk over the side of the boat, and dropped it roughly on the bottom. Miguel's elbow jabbed me in the chest. Pain shot across my ribs but I bit my tongue to keep still.

The soldiers argued. Miguel whispered that one of them did not want to abandon the search for us in the woods; the other wanted to take the pirate on board the ship.

Pinpricks of daylight shone through the corners of the lid

where it did not seal. I breathed a little easier. Despite our confinement, at least we would not suffocate.

By the time the longboat reached the brigantine, the rain was pouring down in sheets, the sound beating against the trunk in waves. The longboat rocked back and forth as the soldiers hoisted the trunk up with ropes, deposited it on the deck, and lashed the handles to the side of the ship. The storm grew in strength. The brigantine rolled with the ocean swells. Thunder cracked overhead.

"The crew has gone below deck. I hear no enemy voices," whispered Miguel after a long silence.

Until now, we dared not speak. "It appears so or they stand like mute statues in the rain."

Lifting my axe from my belt, I slipped the blade between the lid and trunk where it did not seal. A wall of rain bounced along the deck. Miguel pushed his ear to the side of the trunk, listening.

"The prisoners sit in the middle of the deck, tied together in a circle," I whispered. "Rain hits them like a waterfall. Their heads are down. The soldiers have taken refuge in the decks below. Ranson lies close to the prisoners, tied to the winch. He is unconscious. Or dead. I cannot tell."

I pulled back from the edge of the trunk. The time to act was now, but Ranson had to free us first. He could only do that after he freed himself, and at the moment he could not free anybody. Our plan had failed already. My heart grew heavy.

Light flashed through the crack as streaks of lightning filled the sky. Thunder followed and the storm intensified, darkening the sky to night. It rained and rained and rained. We could do nothing but wait. Once the storm lessened and the sun broke through a clearing sky, the crew returned to the deck. They moved along the deck at a hurried pace.

Ear against the side, Miguel made sense of their words. "The water level has risen high enough for the brigantine to move closer to shore . . . they must be quick or the water will recede and they will be stranded . . . the *capitán* orders the crew to prepare . . . they deliver the sixteen-pound cannon and mortar."

Panic pushed against my head. All of this had been for naught if the heavy artillery left the boat. I squeezed my temples, trying to think. Looking at Ranson's motionless body, I prayed he would wake. Instead, two soldiers untied Ranson from the winch and dragged him down the steps to the deck below where, I suspect, they relocated him with the other prisoners. His lifeless head had bobbed on his shoulders as he passed.

I strained to follow what happened next when a body suddenly moved in front of the trunk and pulled the latch open. Miguel turned his quarter-pike toward the opening. I rested my hand on my axe handle. The person shouted at someone in the distance.

Miguel translated. "*Capitán*, I'll just take of care of this here fella . . . when I'm finished . . . you boys will dine on alligator stew and have a big piece of meat to sink yer teeth into."

"Beattie," yelled the *capitán*, "you get over here and help Abrams, now! There is no time to waste."

Beattie stepped away from the trunk, cursing under his breath. Careful not to raise the lid too high, I watched as crewmembers ran back and forth across the deck, shouting directions. They hoisted the artillery up from the cargo hold and secured it with rope lines. Then they lowered a longboat full of crewmembers into the choppy waters.

"What happens now, Pedro?" whispered Miguel.

"They pull the anchors up, ready to steer the ship closer to shore. The crew will row out to the beach and set up a pulley that reaches from the shore to the deck. The gun of the cannon weighs tons and the rope must be strong. They will hoist the barrel of the cannon up from the cargo hold and slide it across the rope to the beach, on a pallet. They will do this with the cannonballs and mortar also. It will not take long."

Miguel took his turn looking out of the corner.

I tucked my axe back inside my belt. "Part of the crew is on the beach; the others attend to the cargo hold. The trunk latch is open and we sit next to the ship's galley. You slip into the kitchen when the time comes. I will follow when I can."

The mortar rose out of the cargo hold first; next came the wooden base of the cannon. While the men looked down inside the cargo hold, I raised the lid high enough for Miguel to squeeze through. He slipped quickly over the side and out.

Then something happened below deck and a group of soldiers ran down the steps. Every soldier turned to watch. I slipped quickly from the trunk to join Miguel in the galley. We craned our necks trying to see.

Two figures backed up the steps toward the deck, one holding the other by a knife. The soldiers on deck moved toward them in a closed circle with their weapons drawn.

"LITTLE BIRD, where are you?" yelled Ranson from inside the circle. The blade of his knife pushed against the *capitán's* back. "Your assistance is greatly needed!"

I stepped out into the open, holding my axe in one hand and my knife in the other. Miguel held his quarter-pike in front of him. "We are both here."

Ranson turned his head toward me, his eyes alive with excitement. "Glad to see you and your little friend are still alive. I feared all was lost. Tie up the crew, good and tight. Make sure to use a granny knot so they don't twist those buggers apart. If they so much as sneeze, I will introduce their *capitán* here to ten lashes with my cat-o'-nine-tails and then send him to Davy Jones's locker at the bottom of the sea. If he doesn't fancy that, we will keelhaul him."

Ranson pressed his knife under the *capitán's* throat. A trickle of blood rolled down his neck. Muttering under his breath, the *capitán* said something in English and the crew lowered their weapons and backed away.

Ranson nodded at the steps leading below deck. "When you've finished that, free the prisoners and bring them upstairs. And be quick about it. The tide will be moving out soon. I will entertain the *capitán* so he does not get bored."

The crew sat motionless on the ground while we tied their hands together. They whispered threats in English and glared at us with eyes full of hate, but their words meant nothing to me. I answered with a smile which vexed them further. When a particularly bad-mannered sailor spat at me, I replied by pinching him so hard on the cheek that he cursed at the top of his lungs.

I turned slowly to survey the crew, the sea, and the beach. The sky had cleared and the sails swung in the air overhead, but toward land, the longboat had disappeared from sight. "Hurry, Miguel, go downstairs and free the prisoners. Take them to Ranson. I will join you soon."

I moved along the sides of the deck, searching for the longboat. If it had pulled up against the hull, it would have been visible. I saw only the sea crashing against the body of the ship. It had not moved to the other side of the hull either.

Then I noticed that the men on the beach had moved into the trees, where they watched the brigantine. Did they drag the longboat into the woods with them? No. There were no drag marks in the sand. Did they carry the longboat away, and if so, where?

I looked at Ranson. The *capitán,* now blindfolded and gagged, was strapped to the mainmast beside him. Ranson stood before the released prisoners, demonstrating how to man the sails.

I looked up. The crow's nest stood overhead. Placing my foot inside the netted rope, I moved quickly up the ladder. Inside the basket lay a field glass. Placing the looking part up to my eye, I moved the magnifying end slowly across the water. The cold winds pounded the crow's nest and the rough and choppy sea rocked the boat. As careful as I was to cover every inch of sea, I could not find the longboat. This worried me.

Turning the lens toward the beach, I looked for groups of unusual footprints where they had carried the heavy longboat. I found none. Then I noticed a soldier hidden inside the trees, gesturing toward the ocean. I quickly swung the field glass around.

That's when I found it. The longboat had passed the brigantine when we were busy tying the crew to the deck. It passed the sea on the other side of the woods, where the coastline curved in. Only a person in the crow's nest could see the ocean on the other side of the woods. My heart jumped inside my chest. The longboat headed toward the enemy ships anchored outside of the Castillo.

Wrapping my legs around the rope ladder, I slid down the twisted rope until I stood upright on the deck. Ranson stood port side studying the horizon. I ran toward him. "The longboat passes out to sea where the enemy is anchored."

He held his hand out, waiting for me to pass him the field glass. "How far is she?" He placed the lens expertly to his eye.

"She is out of range of our muskets." My heart pounded. "But not of our cannons."

"No cannons, Little Bird." He analyzed the location of every enemy vessel. "They would alert the other ships and a Castillo that thinks we are the enemy. We need to sink that longboat long before the enemy is aware of our deeds. If I had my old crew and my blunderbuss, I'd say let the enemy try and take us, but that is not so. I am the *capitán* of two young lads and five land-lovers. No, we are going to intercept the longboat once the sails are in position. They cannot outrun my fine beauty, here. Go! I can manage the ship without you. If I need help, I'll just recruit a few of those English lads with the cutlass the *capitán* has very generously bequeathed to me. Quickly now."

His eyebrows rose high above his eyes, waiting for me to make my move.

I looked questioningly at Miguel. He looked hopeful. I drew in a deep breath and looked down. As much as I wanted to go with the pirate, our duty was with the town. "Go with God's speed, Andrew Ranson. I will look for you when the siege is over."

27

Bandoliers and Flintlocks

*When you engage in actual fighting, if victory is long
in coming, then men's weapons will grow dull
and their ardor will be damped. If you lay siege
to a town, you will exhaust your strength.* — Sun Tzu

MIGUEL AND I SANK the brigantine's raft after coming ashore so it would
not fall into enemy hands. Instead of heading back to the Castillo,
where our path would cross the enemy during daylight, I led us
inside the woods close to the shore. With Ranson in charge of the
brigantine, our urgent need to return to the Castillo had lessened.
My stomach growled in anticipation of a well-deserved meal.

I saw no signs of danger as we moved quietly through the
woods into a well-hidden cove where the low tide exposed a mud-
flat full of oysters. A thick wall of brush shielded us from view as we
began to extract the oysters. I chipped at the shells with the edge of
my axe and Miguel used his quarter-pike to jab them free. We gathered a large pile of oysters before starting the harder task of prying
them open. Miguel stood guard while I used my knife to split the
shells in half.

We anxiously raised the half shells up to our mouths and let
the oysters slide down our throats. As we ate, a large stack of shells
gathered at our feet. The sun had moved midway across the horizon by the time we finished. Miguel patted his full stomach and
grinned. I, too, nodded. To fill our stomachs in the middle of a hungry enemy was an unexpected victory.

Wiping the remnants of my meal against my sleeve, I pointed
toward the Nombre de Dios. "Now, we must learn of any new troop
movements for the garrison."

Miguel grinned. "I anticipated your plan. My thoughts are the
same. I have already counted the stones in my pouch. There are many."

"You are more amenable when your stomach is full," I said.

He slapped me hard on the back. "As are you, my friend."

"This time *my friend,* do not engage the enemy. They would not have given chase if you had not stopped to play with the horses. We seek only to listen and gather information."

Miguel smiled. "And you watch the ground so you are not tempted to fly through the air like a bird with no wings."

Giddy with laughter, we carried on, pointing out each other's folly. Alone in the secluded woods, we welcomed the opportunity to breathe freely and without worry. Our stomachs were full and the pirate had charge of the guns threatening the fort. Despite the rough start, the day was good.

Our happiness was not to last. Voices coming from the direction of the Nombre de Dios changed everything. We backed into the scrub and hid. I slid my bow along the ground beside me until the brush hid it from view. Miguel did the same with his quarter-pike. Breathing as quietly as I could, I waited with my axe at my side.

Deep in conversation, three English soldiers, each carrying a flintlock, appeared from the other side of the thicket. One held a basket in his hands. Miguel translated in a whisper so soft I strained to make out the words.

"What do we have here?" asked the red-headed commander, pointing to the empty oyster shells.

The soldier closest to where we hid answered. "It appears someone has been nicking the food."

"Zimmerman does not complain of hunger and he leaves the mission often. We now see that he fills his own stomach with oysters and keeps it a secret for himself."

The third soldier slammed his fist into his hand. "We'll take care of him when we get back. If Moore won't command his soldiers to obey, then we will. The disobedient and cowardly have nothing to fear from our great leader. They eat the food, steal the treasure, squander the ammunition, and do nothing but complain. Moore does nothing about his disobedient ranks."

The one carrying the basket placed it on the ground. "Hardtack and salt fish stick in my throat and my empty stomach grows weary. I will eat now. Let the others be hanged." He reached into the water to chip off an oyster, but suddenly jerked his hand free. Blood dripped off the ends of his fingers.

The commander threw him a piece of cloth. "Patience, Crawford. Those shells are sharp. Watch where you put your hands. Our orders are to return with food, not return injured."

The three soldiers leaned their flintlocks against the tree trunk, tips up, and laid their bandoliers away from the water. Before beginning the task of extracting oysters from the water, they stopped to roll their sleeves up. When they faced the water, we saw only their backs.

I stared at the flintlocks, a weapon superior to the garrison's old muskets. When the hammer of a flintlock strikes the flint mounted on the barrel, the spark ignites the gunpowder inside the pan and fires off a shot.

Gunpowder loaded into a musket needs to be lit by hand with a burning piece of matchcord. If the weather is damp, the cord or gunpowder may not light and the enemy can see the smoldering red tip of the cord at night, exposing the musketeers where they stand.

I counted a dozen chargers attached to the bandoliers—long leather sashes worn across the chest. Each charger held single shots of gunpowder ready to be loaded. I grinned. A weapon without gunpowder cannot shoot.

The soldier nearest to us pried an oyster open. "The strength of the Spanish Castillo surprises Moore. Grimley reports the trenches are only a musket shot away from the Castillo but the workers flee because they fear the Spanish garrison. The Spanish bombard the workers with bullets and yell, 'Kill! Kill!' to frighten them away. They say the workers are so scared that the Spanish only need to yell, 'Kill! Kill!' and the workers run. Grimley requests that the regiment guard the trenches or the workers cannot finish, but the regiment does not want to be shot and refuses to do so."

The commander placed his oysters in the basket. "My contacts report that they have dug man-made caves inside the trenches to hide in and gabions line the ground above the trenches so the Spanish cannot take aim so easily at the workers. The regiment readies the cannons to move into the trenches. We breach the walls any day now."

Breach the walls. My heart quickened at hearing those words, but I dared not move. Fighting an unbearable urge to run, I drew in a long slow breath and held it. I did this many times to slow my racing heart, a technique I mastered long ago when hunting dangerous prey. It is the mind that steadies the body and a fool who leaps without thinking. I struggled to remember this.

The third soldier tossed an oyster in the basket. "My sources say Grimley was shot last night when his workers came under fire and they ran away. Those that have not been shot are insubordinate and refuse to return to the trenches."

"Give those workers to me!" snarled the soldier closest to us. "I will make them work. We wait for incompetent fools to finish their jobs. We starve while they flee. And how long must we wait for reinforcements to come from Jamaica? Moore promised us an easy victory."

I nodded to myself. Hunger and discontent plagued the enemy. This news would be welcomed. Unfortunately, it was the same at the Castillo. Morale was low. Reinforcements had not arrived. The town's survival depended on the ship *La Gloria*. We did not know if she had reached Cuba or sat on the bottom of the ocean. Rations of food grew smaller each day. Our store of munitions grew less with each encounter, and the constant threat of an enemy breaching the walls exhausted the will of the people. The priests offered prayers of hope, but when help did not come, the mood returned to feelings of despair. Every day the Castillo did not receive reinforcements was a day of victory for the English.

While the soldiers talked, I crawled slowly across the ground on my hands and knees toward the bandoliers. Using a stick to drag the first bandolier slowly toward me, I passed it to Miguel who moved it safely inside the thicket. We moved the other two bandoliers into the thicket in the same fashion.

The hardest task was yet to come. The flintlocks stood out in the open, some distance from the thicket. If the soldiers turned around, I would be exposed like a duck sitting in a pond. But the men were so hungry that they thought only of their stomachs and moved further into the mudflats where the oysters were plentiful. Clearing the brush, I crept quietly across the ground unnoticed.

They did not look up, unaware that we watched every action and listened to every word.

I slid the first flintlock carefully across the ground. It was heavy and hard to steady and I struggled to pull the barrel quietly toward me. I questioned the wisdom of attempting such a task until an argument broke out amongst the men and I took full advantage of the distraction by pulling the other two flintlocks into the brush with me.

28

Back into the Castillo

*It is a matter of life and death, a road either to safety
or to ruin. Hence it is a subject of inquiry which
can on no account be neglected.* — Sun Tzu

FIFTEEN-POUND FLINTLOCKS measuring five foot lengths are awkward
and burdensome beasts to maneuver through trees and brush without noise. We abandoned the third flintlock halfway through our
journey back to the fort when we stopped to gather herbs and cut
wood for a new bow. I slid it under a thicket of saw palmetto bushes
and notched a nearby tree so I could find it later.

We did not hide at the marsh's edge for very long before a
group of townspeople entered the water to cut grass for the dwindling amount of cattle. The small group of women and four soldiers arrived just before dusk. We joined them on their return to
the Castillo.

A canopy of stars hovered above the open courtyard. Glad-
dened by Miguel's and my safe return, Grandmamma and my
mother took the herbs from the pouch and set out to make treat-
ments for the injured. Troubled by recent events inside the Castillo,
their words were few.

The enemy had increased its attack on the garrison, leaving
many wounded. Rounds of musket fire erupted from the gun deck
above us. Children, eyes wide with fear, huddled next to their parents. Many gathered at the small chapel, where a long line of troubled parishioners overflowed into the courtyard. Some cried softly
to themselves while others stood in silence.

Grandpapa waited eagerly for us to visit him in the soldier's
quarters. Anxious to deliver my news of the enemy, I took my place
on the straw mattress next to him. Warmth from the hearth surrounded us. Miguel left to see his family.

"My news of the enemy is grave," I said, "but first I must know what has happened since our departure. There are many long faces inside the courtyard."

Grandpapa's tired eyes searched my face. He had waited hours to hear of my return. "Enemy trenches are within reach of Castillo walls. Their gabions prevent the garrison from stopping them. The enemy is now close enough to fire upon anyone entering the Castillo and the helpers in the marsh. This afternoon, the number of soldiers firing upon the trenches was doubled so a small party could brave the marsh and gather grass."

"That is how I was able to enter the fort," I said.

Grandpapa patted me on the hand. "You were fortunate, Pedro. That may be the last time our messengers can leave the fort and we can gather food for the cattle."

A cannon shot above us.

I twisted around, looking for signs of trouble outside the room's small window. "Why do the cannons fire?"

"They fire on a brigantine. It has steered close to the Castillo and sails within cannon range."

"What!" I jumped up. "No! That is the pirate Ranson. He saves the Castillo by steering the brigantine away from the enemy. That ship carries heavy artillery. We must stop them before they push him into the hands of the English."

I left the officers' quarters and ran up the plank leading to the gun deck where smoke from the cannons blanketed the air.

Cousin Nico blocked my entrance to the battlements. I looked past his pinched face toward the brigantine. The inexperience of the ship's crew was evident. The brigantine moved awkwardly through the water, dipping and swaying as one sail flapped in the breeze and the other sail pulled away from the mast. Ranson had been in need of my help but had not demanded it of me. And I had not been wise enough to see that his need was great.

Unconcerned as to why I was there, Nico punched me hard in the shoulder. "Leave, Pedro. Only soldiers on the gun deck."

I pushed him back. He locked onto my arms. "Let me go, Nico! I have important news for the sergeant."

"You tell me. You are NOT a soldier!"

My face grew hot. I rammed into his side. He stood his ground. I kicked his legs. He pushed me to the ground. I moved out from under his grip and stood up. He crouched down to tackle me, but I grabbed hold of his head and flipped him over. He wriggled free and flipped me over. Nico had grown stronger and had learned a few new tricks since the beginning of the siege.

But so had I. I rammed into his stomach with my head. He fell over backwards, grunting. I moved toward the sergeant, but Nico held on to my ankles and tripped me. I punched him in the side, but he held me by the hair.

Another cannon fired.

I slipped out from under his grip to see the cannonball hit the sail and catch it on fire. My heart moved up to my throat. "Stop! The brigantine fights for the Spanish Crown!"

Nico tackled me from behind. We both fell face down on the deck. I twisted around and latched onto his chest, squeezing the air out of him. He struggled but I held tight. "You win, Nico. I will tell you if you promise to deliver my message to the sergeant NOW."

Then I released him. We both crawled to our feet.

His nostrils flared. His eyes became slits. "Tell me and then get off the gun deck."

I pointed to the sea. "Ranson commandeers the brigantine. He carries the enemy's heavy guns away from the Castillo. We cannot push her into English hands."

Nico stared, his eyebrows high on his forehead. "And how do you know this?"

"Because I helped him take the ship. Hurry."

Nico scoffed. "Liar. I will not fill the sergeant's ears with such madness." He pushed me away.

I pushed him back. "I will pull the ears off your head and feed them to the pigs if you do not tell the sergeant."

The top of his lip curled into a sneer. "You are welcome to try, little cousin."

An anger that I have never felt before boiled up inside of me like a volcano. I clenched my fists so hard that it numbed my fingers, but I could not risk the safety of the brigantine on my desire to pummel my cousin into dust. Breathing rapidly in and out, I tried to center my thoughts. Nico glowered. The urge to hit him was so strong, I had to look away.

The brigantine leaned to the side. The ship teetered at the edge of the cannon's firing range. The sail was now fully ablaze. Without her sails, the ship would drift into full range of the Castillo's armory.

I looked at Nico. "I stole a flintlock from the enemy and I will give it to you in exchange for passing my message to the sergeant."

Nico's smirk disappeared. "You have no flintlock. Show it to me first."

My hands flew up. "There is no time, Nico. I swear on Grandpapa's life. Deliver my message to the sergeant."

Another cannon took aim at the brigantine. It fell just short of hitting the hull. The ship rocked back and forth in the water.

My stomach twisted into a knot. "Now, Nico. Or I swear, on my father's grave, you will regret it."

Nico relented, but he took his time moving toward the sergeant, his walk both measured and with no since of urgency. Glancing over his shoulder at me, he smiled, knowing full well the great anxiety consuming me.

The sergeant looked at me while Nico spoke. If Nico thought to discredit me, he underestimated my relationship with the sergeant and our earlier encounter with the spies in the woods.

The sergeant ordered the cannons to stop. Nico shook his head in disbelief when the garrison set their cannon load to the side. I ran through the smoke to the wall, my eyes and nose stinging under the foul gunpowder. Ranson showed his mastery as a seaman when the brigantine managed to drop its burning sail into the water.

Then we witnessed the main sail swing into position and the billowing sail flap in the wind. Steady in the choppy waters, the brigantine maneuvered around the other ships and headed north into the open sea. I punched at the air and screamed in victory.

29

The Enemy Grows Near

Hence to fight and conquer in all your battles is not supreme excellence; supreme excellence consists in breaking the enemy's resistance without fighting. — Sun Tzu

AFTER THE BRIGANTINE'S NARROW ESCAPE, I returned to Grandpapa's side and told him the story of the spies, Ranson, and the soldiers' conversation at the oyster bed. He called for Uncle Manuel and I was ordered to repeat every detail. Forehead wrinkled with worry, my uncle left to report these events to the governor. I returned to the courtyard, where I barely noticed the stars above before drifting into sleep.

The days stretched on. The garrison continued to take aim at the enemy and those working in the trenches. Restlessness filled my nights. I tossed and turned in my sleep, my feet and legs kicking wildly. Grandmamma stroked my head and whispered in a soothing voice, trying to calm my restless soul.

In my dreams, the enemy drove cannon after cannon into the trenches. I pushed against the iron beasts, but they rolled over top of me as if I were an insect. When the men breached the Castillo's walls, they dragged me inside the Castillo to watch. The words "the trenches are only a gunshot away" echoed inside my head, causing me to relive the same dream over and over again. Each day I woke exhausted and weary.

This day, I did not wake like the others with the crowing of the rooster. The sun was high in the sky by the time the bells from the chapel woke me. Somber faces, surrounded by breaths of cold crisp air, stared as I pulled the covers over my head to block the freezing winds blowing in from the ocean. I rubbed my hands briskly together, trying to warm my frozen fingers.

Juan Felipe made his way toward me.

"Pedro, we need your help. It has been some time since we have spoken. You have been very busy, my friend. Many say the stories of you outside the Castillo are falsehoods but I suspect they are true."

He patted me on the back when I sat up and yawned. "What is it that you need, Juan Felipe?"

He took a seat next to me. "You must collect anything made of metal for the blacksmith: silver, pewter, tin, lead, bronze, iron. Leave one pot for every five families so they may continue to cook over an open flame. Do not gather any type of weapon. We may have need of them soon."

I pulled my axe close.

The expression on Juan Felipe's face was one of grave concern. "We must melt the metal into musket balls. Our supply of musket balls grows critical and we have no hope of replenishing them until help arrives. I will not say 'if help arrives' because those words poison the spirit."

I rubbed my eyes. "Do we also collect the jewelry?" I thought back to when Miguel and I risked our lives to retrieve his mother's necklace from the enemy scout inside town. And there was my own mother and the family heirlooms she had inherited. She did not trade them during the hardest of times. Those trinkets seemed so important then.

"We collect only the metal jewelry. No cloth, beads, or things made of wood. Jewelry exists only to adorn the body but it is musket shot that will stop the enemy and keep the people safe. Remind the people of this if it troubles them."

Grandmamma handed me a goblet of herbal tea and a hard-boiled chicken egg while I shook my drowsy head. "How soon must I bring these things to the blacksmith?"

"Now, Pedro. The garrison prepares for an assault on the rows of gabions closest to the curtain wall tonight. If the garrison destroys the gabions, we will have a clear shot at anyone inside the trenches. We must attempt this or the enemy will be able to breach the walls this very night."

A heavy weight pressed against my heart as I gathered two large, cloth sacks. Sipping the last drop of tea from inside our pewter goblet, I placed it inside the sack.

The mood inside the courtyard was somber. People placed their bracelets, necklaces, buttons, clasps, hinges, door handles, eating knives, spoons, forks, metal chains, hooks, buckets, goblets, chests, treasure boxes—anything made of metal—inside the sacks. They did so with eyes filled with tears.

Lifting the heavy sacks over my shoulder tired my back, but I made my way steadily toward the blacksmith, where I deposited the bags next to the others at the door. Inside, the blacksmith cut the metal into bits before heating the scraps over burning coals, where they melted into pools of liquid metal.

A native Indian, one that I had never seen before, held the mold while the blacksmith poured the hot liquid into the hollowed-out center of a musket-ball mold. When the hot liquid touched the cool metal, it turned at once from a shiny liquid to a gray solid. Then the Indian opened the mold and a musket ball rolled out. He lifted the ball, still hot to the touch, with a pair of tongs and dropped it into a bucket of water, where it cooled down. A stack of musket balls grew on the bottom of the bucket.

When the blacksmith came my way, I asked him about the Indian. "Who is the newcomer?"

"Several families have come into the fort in the last few days seeking asylum. The Yamasee, Juan Lorenzo, arrived early this morning with his family. His wife, baby, and little girl stay with my wife. We are in great need of his blacksmithing skill. The garrison keeps all able hands busy."

I studied the Indian as he hammered the contents of the cloth sacks into smaller pieces. There was a time when the Yamasees had been loyal to Spain; perhaps not all had changed allegiances. He pounded a round goblet flat before chipping away at the metal. His eyes did not stray from his task, nor did he try to engage the other natives coming into the shop in conversation. Skill such as his was uncommon.

Grandpapa would have reminded me that if someone was in real need of sanctuary, we as a people cannot deny our humanity and turn them away. Feeling some comfort in those words, I turned away from the shop and headed toward my family campsite.

Grandmamma sat close to the fire, using a stick to stir the broth brewing inside a pot allotted to our family and four others for cooking. When it had stewed to her satisfaction, she poured the contents into a wooden bowl. Our neighbor carried the pot away as soon as Grandmamma finished.

She patted the seat next to her. "Your grandpapa sleeps today. His mind slips in and out of childishness. My heart aches for him. He prays that the Almighty will not call him, so he may see us through this. He is anxious that we remain safe."

A tear rolled down Grandmamma's check. A knot formed in my throat. Consumed with the actions of the enemy, I had not given thought to my grandfather's inner struggles. I had grown comfortable, thinking he would be with us forever. The knot inside my throat tightened.

Grandmamma sensed my uneasiness. "How do you fare today, grandson?"

Words stuck in my throat. "I'm . . . I'm tired from fighting all night in my sleep."

"The soldiers are plagued with the same problem. They fight in their sleep and cannot find rest. I fear it will only get worse."

I rubbed my temples. "Do you request anything of me, Grandmamma? I must go visit Grandpapa. Perhaps his mind has cleared."

She looked away. "Perhaps today will be a good day."

Tears filled Grandmamma's eyes but she did not want me to see how she suffered. Her teary eyes searched through her many pouches and containers.

"I must have more roots and herbs or our soldiers will die of infection. Many are wounded and our needs have grown beyond our supply, even though you have been faithful in gathering what you can. You must ask the others for ginger root, garlic, and onion for these, too, help the body fight infection. I need willow bark for pain, witch hazel to clean the wounds, and elderberry for congestion. The time for the passionflower has passed, but if anyone has the dried blossoms, bring them to me. I will make a tea to help the sleepless and wounded relax."

I reached for my pouch. "I will go into the woods and fetch those things for you. Miguel and I will go together. With his help I will be able to carry twice—"

Before I could finish, Uncle Manuel, who had just arrived, interrupted. "Mother, it is not safe for Pedro to go outside the fort's walls. The danger is too great now."

Grandmamma wiped her eyes against her sleeves and looked up. "I know this, Manuel. Your mother would not ask her grandson to take such a risk. I was about to instruct him to ask the others here in the Castillo." She turned toward me, her eyes brimming with tears again. "Pedro, I am in need of moss and cattail too."

I turned toward my uncle. "The danger has been great all along, Uncle. I will do what is needed of me. If Grandmamma deems it necessary, then I return to the woods."

He did not smile. "I have no doubt of this nephew, but the enemy descends on the fort in great numbers. They are able to shoot anyone going into the marsh. There is no safe place to run and no place to hide. My brother, God rest his soul, would not want me to risk the life of his youngest son on a fool's errand."

I straightened my back, standing as tall as possible. "I must go, Uncle, or many will suffer."

"Just as your life will suffer when the enemy has relieved you of it. My decision is final, Pedro." He looked at me, his expression troubled. "Your grandpapa, my own father, who brings me to task as well as you, would agree that the need is great but the time is not right."

Folding my arms in protest, I sat down.

My uncle bent down to look directly in my eyes. "Obey my command, Pedro. I am leading a sally of infantry to destroy the rows of gabions growing closest to the curtain wall this very night. This will be a dangerous task. The soldiers must carry torches so they can see the work before them, but it will make us visible to the enemy. You will not have coverage to enter the woods and the enemy will be traveling through the same woods in great numbers. Our concern cannot be for your safety."

I sighed. "I will do what is right, Uncle." My eyes drifted in the direction of the trenches. "Can Miguel and I watch the garrison from the gun deck?"

He rubbed his chin in thought. "I suppose you and Miguel have earned the privilege. Perhaps this will satisfy your curiosity. Stay away from the guns and do not interfere."

For the first time in days, a small smile crossed my lips. "Do not worry, Uncle. The garrison will not know we are there."

30

The Gunpowder Room

*The enemy's spies who have come to spy on us must
be sought out, tempted with bribes, led away and
comfortably housed. Thus they will become
converted spies and available for our service.* — Sun Tzu

GRANDPAPA SLEPT SOUNDLY while I placed another log on the fire inside the officers' quarters. The surrounding air smelled of burning pine and warmed the chill from my own face and hands. I pulled the blanket up around his head and tucked the edges inside.

Despite my efforts to let him sleep, his eyes opened. "Manuel, has the enemy been caught? They enter the Castillo unheeded."

My heart sank. "It is Pedro, Grandpapa. Uncle Manuel is with the garrison planning their attack on the gabions."

Grandpa's wild eyes searched my face. "Do not trust them, Manuel! They hide their true intentions from us. They come into the Castillo under false pretenses."

I stroked his hair. "It is Pedro, Grandpapa. I do not know of what you speak."

He tossed his head back and forth, thoroughly agitated. "Catch them, Manuel, or they will destroy us."

My throat tightened as I said words that did not hold meaning. "Do not worry. We will catch them."

Grandpapa stopped thrashing and stared off into the distance. It was some time before he spoke again. "Then we are safe? Our family lives?"

I stroked his hair. "Yes, we are safe. The family lives."

Then he slowly closed his eyes, released the grip from my arm, and fell back to sleep.

My heart tugged at my insides as a gut-wrenching sadness overcame me. The days of Grandpapa being himself have been many. Now, as much as ever, I needed his insights and his wisdom. But most important, he has been the one to guide me and teach me since my father's death many years ago. Everything I do is because he has shown me the ways of a man.

I whispered, praying he would somehow understand the meaning in my words. "Sleep well, Grandpapa. You are safe here inside the officers' quarters. You have taught me that the enemy does not view a young boy as much a threat as a soldier. I will use that to our advantage when the opportunity presents itself. If I lose my life to the enemy, know that I love you and I do this for the family. I do what you have taught me to do as a man."

Then I wiped the tear from my eye, kissed him on the forehead, and left.

✳✳✳

AFTER THE SUN WENT DOWN, Miguel joined me on the gun deck, his flintlock and quarter-pike at his side. I carried my bow and axe. Quiet surrounded us. The cannons sat idle as the soldiers patrolled the battlements.

The most experienced soldiers gathered in the courtyard, ready for a raid on the line of gabions closing in on the Castillo walls. Uncle Manuel gave orders and checked weapons. The men held unlit torches and carried muskets, picks, and machetes, waiting for the gate to lower. Clouds of breath hung in the cold night air around them.

It was quiet outside the walls, the enemy unaware of the pending attack. A quarter moon showed in the clear night sky.

"What is our plan, Pedro?" asked Miguel.

"We will watch from the gun deck. The gate will remain open so the men are able to retreat quickly."

He nodded his understanding. Once the bridge was down, the men lit their torches, advanced across the bridge, and disappeared around to the west side of the fort. Gunfire broke out as the men approached the wall of gabions running northwest to east.

Working in twos, the Spanish infantry pushed the gabions over, spilling the dirt and stones into the bottom of the trench. This action served two purposes. It destroyed the wall of gabions, allowing the garrison to put the enemy in their sights, and it deposited mounds of rocks and debris across the ground so their cannons could not pass.

The enemy fired on the infantry with such intensity that despite the barrage of musket fire returning from the Castillo, the speed of the infantry's work was gruelingly slow.

Then the enemy singled out the men wielding picks and axes by pointing their flintlocks at them. The soldier closest to the enemy line lay dead. Others were gravely injured, but many, crippled with wounds, continued to tear the baskets apart and set them ablaze with fire. Gunshots from the San Pablo and San Pedro bastions blasted the enemy with crossfire, but it was not enough to stop the attack. Smoke blanketed the air, making it difficult to see.

Miguel and I shifted nervously from our positions on the wall. Juan Felipe screamed at us from the San Pablo bastion. "Pedro, we need more gunpowder! Pronto!"

We ran down the ramp and crossed the courtyard toward the powder magazine in the northeast corner room. Babies cried. Many of the people, huddled together in small groups, buried their heads in their arms.

As soon as we reached the door to the powder magazine, we stopped. The guard was missing and the door stood ajar. Miguel and I gazed at each other in alarm. With so many outsiders and strangers inhabiting the Castillo, guarding the powder magazine was one of the garrison's primary duties.

We looked around the door into a dim interior. Propped against the stone wall stood a small candle burning inside a glass globe. A shadow fell across the small group of wooden budge barrels stacked in the corner of a room once full of ammunition. To the untrained eye, the small copper-hooped budge barrels do not appear to be much, but they store the gunpowder needed by the battery of cannons located on the gun deck.

Then we saw the Yamasee Indian, the one the blacksmith called Juan Lorenzo, crouched behind the stack of budge barrels, a knife in one hand and a lit linstock in the other. My heart jumped into my throat. The Yamasee intended to ignite the budge barrels. If that were to happen, the whole room would blow up. The explosion would bring down the walls and the gun deck above us. Then our enemy would march through breached walls fully armed.

Drawing my axe from my belt, I pointed it at Lorenzo's head. "PUT THE LINSTOCK DOWN."

Ignoring my presence, the Yamasee Lorenzo hurried to split the side of a budge barrel with his knife. Gunpowder began to seep out. I squeezed the handle of my axe but did not dare let go. The risk was too great. If the Yamasee dropped the linstock close to the gunpowder, it would ignite. I lunged instead. He parried my move. My shoulder hit the side of the barrel in my fall. The crack widened and the gunpowder poured into large heaps on the floor.

Lorenzo rushed toward the gunpowder. Before I could pull myself up, Miguel pushed his bayonet to the Yamasee's throat. "Stop! Or I will remove your head."

The Yamasee hesitated. I yanked the linstock from his hands and pushed him to the ground. Miguel pushed the tip of his bayonet into the Indian's neck until the skin puckered. Lorenzo let go of his knife. I slid it toward the door and away from the gunpowder. My heart pounded inside my chest.

"What has happened, Pedro?" An elder from a local tribe emerged through the opening.

I stepped on the tip of the linstock and smothered the flame. "The newcomer, Juan Lorenzo, tried to blow up the powder room."

The elder shut his troubled eyes and sighed. Then he opened them again. "We feared as much. Juan Lorenzo seemed sincere but his actions have not been honorable."

My mother and Grandmamma pushed through the door behind the elder and entered the room. Two women from the local tribe stood behind them. It was Grandmamma who spoke. "Go, Pedro. The tribe will turn Juan Lorenzo over to the garrison."

Members of the tribe held the newcomer in place while Miguel and I lifted a budge barrel of black gunpowder carefully from the room and carried it slowly up the ramp to the gun deck. Not wanting to ignite the volatile gunpowder by our carelessness, we avoided the cloud of cinders and embers floating in the air. The gun smoke was so thick at the top of the ramp that we could not see the path before us. The foul air burned our lungs and caused us to cough but we moved with tear-filled eyes toward Juan Felipe, where we managed to lower the budge barrel slowly to the deck. Returning quickly to the powder magazine, we brought two more budge barrels up to the battery the same way.

When the job was finished, we returned to the wall to watch the battle. Much had happened since we were gone. Wounded soldiers lay on the ground writhing in pain. Gabions that had been destroyed with machetes and set on fire filled the trenches. A large group of the enemy had retreated into the woods, their lanterns appearing as fireflies through the trees.

I pointed at the wounded on the ground. "We must help bring in the wounded while the garrison keeps the enemy busy."

Within the short time it took us to clear the gate and reach the infantry, the state of affairs had reversed. English soldiers from the Nombre de Dios joined the ranks and the enemy now advanced on the infantry in the trenches. Sparks from enemy flintlocks flashed across the horizon. Gunfire surrounded us.

A bullet nicked my arm. I slid behind an untouched gabion. A second bullet made a crunching sound when it hit the sand and dirt inside. Two more crunching sounds erupted as the enemy took aim. I looked down to see blood soaking through my tunic.

Our soldiers did not retreat. Those that were not injured continued to dump the contents of the gabions into the trenches and then set the wicker baskets on fire. The musketeers from the Castillo fired at an advancing enemy but the return fire did not lessen.

Miguel fell when a bullet hit his leg. Stepping out into the open, I dragged him to the side of the trench, where I lowered him inside and jumped in after him. We landed on top of a jagged pile of rocks and stack of shovels.

Gunshots fired overhead. Miguel leaned against the wall while I pushed the shovels up to the ground. An enemy without tools could not dig.

He struggled to stand. "We must help the infantry."

I pulled him down. A bullet only inches above his head sprayed dirt into the air.

"A dead man cannot help anyone!"

He pinched his face in pain but did not say more.

Placing an arrow inside my newly carved bow, I waited until

the sound of gunfire had lessened, then I reached above the trench line and let go. The arrow shot straight but where it landed I did not know. Forced to duck below the line again, I released four more arrows in the same fashion, each time ignorant of whether they found a mark. My heart thumped inside my chest.

"Shoot a devil for me, Pedro," shouted Miguel. He pushed his flintlock toward me.

Trading my bow for his flintlock, I struggled to lift its fifteen-pound weight above the wall and clumsily take aim. The blast knocked me backwards. My ears went numb. Like the fate of my arrows, I did not know if the gunshot hit any mark.

I turned toward Miguel, waiting for him to hand me a charger from his bandolier. Once I rammed the barrel with gunpowder and shot, I would not fire again without aim. Every shot needed to count or my presence on the field was for naught.

Miguel looked up from his bandolier, his eyes wide with surprise. "The chargers are empty. We had only the one shot."

I pushed the flintlock toward Miguel and picked up my arrow again. "Then it is true. The enemy grows low on ammunition too."

Just then, a flaming piece of gabion floated off the ground above us and fell inside the trench at our feet. I raised my foot ready to stamp it out, but remembered it must burn or the enemy would fill it again. The flames reached high in the air before dying out. Miguel, using his flintlock as a crutch, stumbled beside me while we climbed further up the trench toward the Castillo's wall.

It was then that I heard horses. I looked up in time to see a small group of soldiers ride out of the Castillo on fast horses, going west toward Apalachee. Our soldiers on the wall cheered when the riders rode safely out of sight.

It was not long before the English regained their lost ground and started advancing slowly toward the trench where Miguel and I hid. Holding only pikes, at the front of the enemy line were the three soldiers from the oyster beds. I could not help smiling at their lack of firearms.

Miguel languished on the ground, blood covering the length of his trousers. When Uncle Manuel gave the signal to retreat, gunfire from the San Pablo, San Pedro, and San Carlos bastions formed a wall of crossfire. We joined the infantry edging toward the port sally. The wounded, helped by those who could walk, used shovels to lean on. Others gathered abandoned firearms scattered across the ground. We crossed the gate into the fort through a rain of fire.

31

Betrayal

The art of war is of vital importance to the State. — Sun Tzu

"**PEDRO, DID I NOT TELL YOU** to stay inside the Castillo?" screamed Uncle Manuel. He sat on the family trunk grimacing while Grandmamma dug shrapnel out of his chest.

Her voice was soothing. "Calm down, Manuel. I must treat your wound or it will fester. Heated words only fuel the temper. That is not good for healing."

Hearing the anger in his voice, I did not feel the need to answer. I tended to my own wound instead, by rinsing it and placing herbs on my arm where the flesh had opened. Many in the infantry were grievously injured and required the help of any who were able. My wound was not life threatening and was of no concern to anyone. Mother attended to Miguel's injured leg on the other side of the courtyard.

"It was Pedro and Manuel who saved the powder magazine from destruction. Be thankful for that," said Grandmamma, "or we would all be dead."

Uncle Manuel winced. "The natives loyal to Spain said they did not trust the Yamasee Juan Lorenzo, but they are warring tribes and will not hesitate to undermine each other. The newcomer claims he heard the garrison call for gunpowder and he sought to help carry the budge barrels to the gun deck."

I stood. "That is a falsehood! He held a lit linstock in his possession and a knife ready to split the barrel open."

Uncle Manuel looked sternly at me. "He says the linstock was already in the room and it was not lit."

"Another falsehood!" I yelled. "He was preparing to light the gunpowder."

"Yes, Miguel reported the same thing. Do not worry, Pedro.

I will get to the truth. My men question him now and they will not stop until they are satisfied that he has nothing to hide. Some say you make up stories to bring glory to yourself."

I crossed my arms, fury growing inside of me. "That is not true. And how is it that the powder magazine was left unguarded?"

"I do not take it lightly that a boy questions me." My uncle glared. "It matters not that you are my brother's son."

Sitting down again, I said nothing more, fearing it unwise to test my uncle further.

Uncle Manuel groaned when Grandmamma used the hot tip of a knife to open the wound. She dabbed at the bleeding wound with a cloth soaked in oak tannin. "Families say you placed your own son, Nico, on guard duty in front of the powder magazine and he abandoned his post."

Uncle Manuel answered through gritted teeth. "There was greater need for him elsewhere."

"Greater need than protecting the powder magazine from strangers inside our Castillo? And who decided this? Nico or the officer in command?" asked Grandmamma as she prodded the inside of his wound.

"Mother, why do you also challenge me?" He squeezed the side of the trunk with his free hand, trying not to cry out.

"Because your father is not here to do so. You know very well, Manuel, that he would ask this of you."

He moaned in pain. "Nico helped load the muskets."

Grandmamma pressed a packet of herbs against the wound. "Nico left his station in front of the powder magazine without instruction and it almost cost us our lives. You are too soft on him, Manuel. Would you have been so forgiving if another soldier had left his post without orders? If it were Pedro instead of Nico?"

Uncle Manuel sighed. "It is his mother's fault that he is so difficult. She babies him."

Grandmamma turned her attention to another wound. "And he has grown mean because of it. And why was the newcomer not in chains? If the Indians loyal to Spain came to you with concerns, why was the Indian not contained during the encounter?"

Uncle Manuel flinched when she pushed against his open

135

flesh. "Because the reports were just suspicions and we do not have time to take care of prisoners. The Indians loyal to Spain were asked to watch him."

I could not hold my tongue any longer. "So, it matters not that Nico allowed the newcomer access to the powder magazine because he prefers to load muskets over protecting our gunpowder?"

My uncle slammed his fist on the side of the trunk. "Do not be insolent, Pedro. I will accept full blame if your story is true, but it appears to me that you are making up stories to embarrass your cousin. You two have a long history of rivalry. This does not excuse you from disobeying me."

I looked down pretending to address my wound. He looked away, sucking in air through gritted teeth as Grandmamma dug at the inside of another wound. During the course of our heated conversation, a soldier appeared out of the crowd to stand in front of Uncle Manuel.

"Sir, we have questioned the prisoner Juan Lorenzo and he refuses to talk. He only states what has been said before."

"Did you use force?" asked my uncle.

"Yes, sir. Even under torture he refuses to talk."

"Do you feel he is hiding something?"

"I do, sir."

Uncle Manuel looked at Grandmamma. "I must go and attend to this. If he is aligned with the enemy, we must know of their treachery."

Grandmamma finished dressing his last wound and he left. As soon as he was out of sight, she stood up, tidied her surroundings, and straightened her clothes. "I must visit the blacksmith's wife."

I prepared to go with her. "That is where the Yamasee's wife and children stay."

"Yes, and while I am asking about the health of the blacksmith's family, I will casually mention that Juan Lorenzo has betrayed the Castillo and is being tortured by the garrison. You must stay here, Pedro. They must not be suspicious of my motives."

"And why would you do this, Grandmamma?"

Grandmamma gave a small smile. "It is not natural for a woman to allow her husband to be tortured and to hear news of his pain. That is all I will say." Then she gathered a small bundle of herbs and left.

32

Forever

*What the ancients called a clever fighter is one who
not only wins, but excels in winning with ease.* — Sun Tzu

MIGUEL, HIS LEG BOUND with a bandage and supported by a wooden
splint, stood uneasily on the gun deck alongside me, observing the
enemy. He tried not to grimace as he struggled to keep his balance.
I knew he was in great pain but would not say so.

English ships sat on the horizon out of range of our cannons.
Hard gusts of freezing wind battered the Castillo. I pulled my tunic closed at the top and buried my hands inside my clothes at the
waist.

It had been five days since the garrison had destroyed the enemy gabions. The risk had been great for the Castillo. Many lay injured inside the fort. Grandmamma attended to the wounded night
and day, her supply of roots and herbs almost exhausted. The need
for me to go into the woods to pick the plants needed was greater
than any time before, but the enemy was too great in number.

A newly reconstructed wall of gabion baskets replaced the
ones decimated by the infantry. Once again, a row of gabions ob-
structed the garrison's ability to stop any movements inside the
trenches as the enemy prepared their cannons for a full-scale attack.
The mood inside the Castillo was one of despair. Many openly wept
and irritable tempers flared. My own heart was heavy with worry.
Our supply of gunpowder and musket balls was critically low.

"Does the governor hold out hope for help?" asked Miguel.

Juan Felipe pointed toward the west where enemy tents
camped. "Because you are almost men, you must hear the truth as
men. I do not believe help will come from the west. The enemy occupies the land and our numbers are small. Our only hope is that *La
Gloria* made it to Cuba and that Havana sends help as requested."

I searched the horizon. "If help does not come soon, it will be too late."

Juan Felipe squeezed my arm. "I fear your words are true."

We bid Juan Felipe farewell and made our way back to the courtyard. Miguel held onto my arm as he limped slowly down the ramp toward the courtyard. His condition filled me with great concern. His face was pale and his voice tired. And he would not heed my words when I asked to gather news of the enemy by myself. I did not require his company for such things and it was more important that he heal.

I held him by the belt to steady his walk. "I want to ask Grandmamma Leena about the fate of the traitor Yamasee, Juan Lorenzo. Come, we must find her."

Miguel sucked in his breath but did not complain as we walked slowly toward the officers' quarters where she attended to my grandpapa. Knowing how much Miguel suffered crushed me. I swallowed, trying to clear the lump from my throat.

"I only regret I cannot help you now," he said.

I smiled. "I would not be standing here today, if not for you my friend."

"Nor I you," he said with a weak smile.

We found Grandmamma at Grandpapa's side. Grandpapa lay covered in blankets on his mattress in front of the fireplace. She lovingly caressed his head.

Grandpapa turned toward me, his eyes alert and his mind clear. "My heart is full of pride, grandson. Your grandmamma tells me all that you and Miguel have done. And you, Miguel, have proven to be every bit a man as Pedro. Providence placed the two of you together."

Miguel reclined slowly onto a nearby bunk. "It has been your guidance that has shown us the way, *Señor*. The Almighty blessed us with you," he said.

"And your tongue has become wise in its choice of words," Grandpapa chuckled.

The hour passed quickly as we laughed and talked of glory. Grandpapa's infectious good spirits warmed our hearts. The warmth radiating from the fire took the chill from the biting winter winds and our weary souls. For a brief time, the enemy did not exist and pending battles were only a distant thought.

When the time was right, I nudged Grandmamma with my shoulder. "Pray tell, what has become of the Yamasee Juan Lorenzo?"

It was Grandpapa who answered. "He did not talk under torture but his wife and daughter came forward and confessed. Lorenzo had entered the fort intent on blowing up the powder magazine for the enemy. Your actions prevented him from doing so."

I punched the air with my fist. "I knew it. And what is Nico's fate for leaving the powder magazine unguarded?"

Grandpapa frowned. "Nico has been relieved temporarily of active duty and is in charge of supervising the latrine."

"Is that all?" I said grumpily. "He should have been permanently relieved of duty." Nevertheless, Miguel and I grinned at each other.

"He is a soldier in the Crown's service, Pedro, and we are in need of men. That is all the governor is willing to do for now," said Grandpapa.

I leaned away from the others to whisper in Grandmamma's ear on another matter. "I have brought Miguel to you. He does not complain but I fear he does not improve."

Her worried face confirmed what I already knew. "His skin is pale, his eyes dull, and his skin hot to the touch. I will take him back to our campsite where I store my supplies. You remain with your grandpapa until sleep overcomes him. Any day now may be his last. Thank the good Lord for allowing him to reach us on this day and that the news is good."

A familiar knot formed in my throat. "I stay with Grandpapa, Miguel. You go with Grandmamma and do what she says."

Before leaving, Grandmamma caressed Grandpapa's forehead, told him how much she loved him, and kissed him lovingly on the check. Then she turned toward Miguel. He did not argue when she took his arm and directed him to toward our campsite. It was then that I knew he suffered more than he let on.

Grandpapa pulled on his covers. "Do not lose hope, grandson. The enemy has not yet won."

I rubbed the back of my neck. "What can we do? The enemy

readies to breach our walls. Our gunpowder is almost gone, we have used all the metal in the Castillo to make musket shot, our food rations grow smaller, and the animals starve in the moat. We have been here almost two months, feed fifteen hundred people each day, and have no hope for supplies. Many of the people are ill with the cold and our soldiers' wounds fester. Christmas draws near but no one celebrates. I fear the Castillo will be a Christmas present to the English."

Grandpapa squeezed my hand. "But we still live, Pedro. The enemy has not taken that from us. They use deception and military strength against us, and we still live. While we still live, there is hope. Be strong and do what you must. Let your heart be your guide. I will always stand with you, grandson, no matter the circumstances. Always know that your grandpapa loves you and is proud of the man you have grown to be. Your papa would feel the same."

I looked at him through watery eyes. "You have been the man in my life. You have taught me all that I know and I love you, Grandpapa."

He patted me gently on the side of the head. I took his hand in mine as he turned and stared off into space. Then he closed his eyes and went to sleep. Forever.

33

Into the Hands of the Enemy

*Hence the skillful fighter puts himself into a position
which makes defeat impossible, and does not miss
the moment for defeating the enemy.* — Sun Tzu

I WOULD NOT LEARN of Grandpapa's passing until two days later. As it was, no one, including Grandmamma, knew of it until later that night when it was time to feed him. If I had known, I would have been so grief stricken that I would not have been able to do what was required of me next. It was providence that I remained ignorant of his death.

I left Grandpapa asleep on his mattress and returned to my family campsite, where I noted Miguel's absence by the time I arrived.

Grandmamma wrung her hands in worry. "Pedro, I fear Miguel's wound is infected and that he may not live the week if I do not have tannin water, garlic, onion, and herbs to treat him."

I sat on the trunk, surprised by the gravity of her words.

She stroked my cheek trying to soothe my troubled soul, just like she did when I was little. "Even if we are able to find those things in the Castillo, our prayers may not be answered."

I leaned back, startled by her words. "Why do you say this?"

She pulled on her hands, fretting openly. "The enemy has not touched the inside of our fort, but its long fingers have done harm nevertheless. Miguel's body burns with fever but his spirit is strong. This is why he could accompany you today. Tomorrow he will not be able to do so. His wound does not close. I must attempt to treat him or he will surely die."

I shook my head, trying to measure her words. "I did not think his wound to be so serious. He is young and strong like a buck."

142

"If a wound festers, it will spread and the body cannot over-come it. This has become Miguel's fate."

A knot formed in my stomach and a feeling of deep remorse came over me. If I had not dragged Miguel into the battle with me, this would not have happened. My insides felt numb. I struggled to swallow.

Grandmamma's forlorn eyes studied me. "I am sorry, Pedro. I know how much he means to you. All we can do now is make him comfortable and do what we can."

I looked up at her, stricken by the finality in her voice. "Do not say this. He is not yet dead!"

She placed her hands on my shoulder. "There is nothing to be done. It is too dangerous to leave the fort, the winter woods do not bear the plants we need, and the governor has forbidden your departure. The cost would be your life for another and that price is too high."

"But it is *I* who forced him to go. It is my fault that he dies."

"No, Pedro, the choice was Miguel's. You did not bind him and drag him there. This is the way of war, grandson. War takes lives, whether on the field or off the field. This will never change."

I brushed her hands away. "I cannot sit here while my friend passes from this world. I will go over the wall tonight on the north-east side of the Castillo next to the marsh. The moon is not yet full and the enemy will not see me if I am careful. Pray that my journey fares well so I may return with what you need."

Before she could reply, I hurried away.

✳✳✳

THAT NIGHT, I paced anxiously next to the lookout tower waiting for Juan Felipe to come with the rope. The night sky was clear and the moon brighter than I expected. It took a long time to convince him to help me, but he agreed after considering the consequences. I carried several canteens, two of them empty, a knife, a large sack, my new bow, and my axe. If the enemy wanted to do me harm, it would not be without a fight. A cloud of breath hung in the air before me.

Most of the garrison faced the west and northwest walls of the Castillo where the English trenches were alive with movement.

The enemy had moved closer to the fort once our soldiers had stopped firing. The garrison possessed only limited gunpowder and now waited for times of urgency. I could not dwell on what was to come. If the enemy was busy with preparations to breach the walls, it would, woefully, work to my advantage.

Juan Felipe moved up the ramp with great haste toward me, holding a coiled rope in his hands. "Make the sound of an owl once you have returned. I will lower the rope. You must return before morning. When the sun begins to rise above the horizon, you will be visible to the enemy. Only the darkness of night keeps you safe for now."

I drew in a deep breath, centering my thoughts. "I understand, Juan Felipe. You are a good friend. I know your brother suffers from his wounds. I will bring back all that I can to help him and the other wounded."

Juan squeezed my shoulder. "I already know this of you, Pedro. You are very much like your father, God rest his soul. Go with God's blessing. You will need it." Then he hitched the rope around the cannon and tossed the remainder over the wall. "Do not hesitate at whatever you do. Make a decision and follow through with skill. Now go, before the garrison notices our deception."

I waited until the musketeers took aim at the enemy standing out in the open before moving across to the marsh wall, where I shimmied down the side of the fort before anyone noticed. When I reached the bottom of the moat, I looked up. Juan Felipe nodded at me from the gun deck. Bending down, I made myself as small as possible and moved slowly out of the ditch, along the border of the marsh, and toward the cover of trees.

Lanterns dotted the tree line and the grounds surrounding the fort. The woods were thick with the enemy. I had never seen so many soldiers. They came for the full-scale attack on the curtain wall, no doubt.

I stopped and listened. Laughter rose from the many campsites. Song filled the air. I heard men grunting under the weight of moving heavy artillery across soft ground. Knowing the woods were not safe, I steered away from the western territory, where the enemy camped in numbers, and moved north along the trees toward the beach, where candlelight and lanterns did not shine.

I had not advanced very far when I heard a noise behind me. Crouching behind the scrub, I pulled my bow from my back and removed the axe from my belt. I parted the bushes to see.

A solitary figure crept along the same path I had just passed. The figure stopped in front of the scrub where I hid and looked around. Recognizing my foe, I drew up out of the scrub, and placed my axe against his neck. "Why do you follow me, Nico?"

He did not answer.

I pushed hard on his neck, the sharpened edge ready to slice the skin. "Answer me or I will tie you up and leave you where the enemy will find you."

The defiance in his voice was unmistakable. "I followed you down the rope when Juan Felipe was not looking. I came to stop you."

His words surprised me. "Stop me from what?"

"You are a traitor and have come to help the English take the Castillo. Just like your father before you."

I drew within an inch of his face. "What madness drives you? I work to save the Castillo, not serve it on a platter to the enemy. And my father never betrayed the Crown."

"Carlos Fernando says your father was killed inside enemy lines because he worked as a spy. The enemy killed him when they discovered he worked for both sides."

It took all my strength to keep from shoving my axe into his throat. "Those words hold no truth. We will question Carlos Fernando in front of Uncle Manuel when I return to the fort. He will not tell falsehoods in front of my father's brother."

"That may be difficult. Carlos Fernando's wounds grow worse. The surgeon is with him now."

I stepped back and placed my axe back inside my belt. "Then I pray that he lives long enough to tell the truth. Return to the fort, Nico, where it is safe. I am here to gather herbs for Grandmamma. You need not concern yourself."

He did not move.

"I said go, Nico." I picked up my bow and positioned it against my back.

Nico moved closer. "I said I am here to stop you."

I looked at him, shaking my head in disbelief. He carried only a dagger. One swipe of my axe would disarm him. "Then you are here to stop me from bringing herbs back to the Castillo to treat the wounded. Help me gather what I need and do not do anything foolish. If you can do this, I will not tie you up. It is your decision."

I folded my arms waiting for his response. It was nighttime but my eyes had adjusted to the dark, and light from the moon illuminated our surroundings. Not wanting to let me out of his sight, Nico agreed to follow me.

Once we entered the heart of the woods far from enemy eyes, it became harder to see. Finding the plants I needed was difficult. I did not relish having Nico for company, but I had hoped two sets of hands would lessen the time it took to gather such a great quantity of plants.

As it turned out, Nico was not much help. He had not learned about herbs or roots and did not understand the outdoors other than making fires and gathering wood. He kept watch while I searched. As much as I did not trust him, necessity forced me to place my safety in his hands.

The season had passed for many of the herbs that I needed, making it necessary that I search for dry leaves still on the stalk. I dug wild onion and garlic bulbs out of the hard ground and filled one of the canteens with standing groundwater dark with tannin. I filled another canteen from a spring smelling of foul sulfur water. The third canteen held fresh water for my own needs, but when the time came, I would pour it out and fill it with tannin water before going back to the fort.

It was during my search that I discovered an English banner partly covered in pine needles and palm fronds.

Nico tugged at it, trying to take it from my hand. "The flag bearer must have dropped it or it fell from their supplies. Give it to me. I will take it back to the fort to remind our soldiers why they fight."

I pulled it back towards me. "You may give it to the garrison once we return. I have need of it."

Nico did not let go. "What need do you have of an English banner?"

I pried his fingers off and offered him my bag. "Take this to Grandmamma. She is in great need of it. Many of the English do not wear uniforms because this is Governor Moore's army, not Queen Anne's of England. It is the same for the banner bearers. If I walk into the enemy camp carrying a banner, they will not have reason to distrust me."

Nico looked at me suspiciously. "It is as I thought. You go to the enemy to betray us. It is saving your own neck that you think of. It is my duty to stop you." He set the sack on the ground and pulled his dagger out.

Anger toward my gullible cousin rose up inside me. But it was providence that kept me from acting upon it because I did not possess such control. Swallowing my disgust instead, my reply came out in tight measured words. "Why would I gather herbs for Grandmamma if I am going to betray us?"

"You did that to fool me, but I know your true intentions."

I shook my head. "If you do not feel my intentions are true, then take my bow and aim it at my heart. Let me walk through the enemy campsite to see what actions they take. Shoot me if I begin to betray us to the English. You know we must bring back news of the enemy or they will not forgive our exit from the Castillo."

My heart pounded as I pushed my new bow toward him. I placed myself in grave danger at the hands of my own cousin.

Nico turned my bow around and pointed it at me. "If you are that foolish, enter the English campsite, little cousin. If your actions are not honorable, I will not hesitate to shoot."

I stooped down, took a handful of dirt from the ground, rubbed it between my hands and smeared it across my clothes, my face, and my hair. Looking more like a battle-worn banner boy than one sitting idle inside the Castillo, I picked up the English banner, stepped out into the open, and walked boldly into the middle of the enemy camp.

34

To Know Fear

Be extremely subtle, even to the point of formlessness. Be extremely mysterious, even to the point of soundlessness. Thereby you can be the director of the opponent's fate. — Sun Tzu

SEVERAL OF THE ENEMY SOLDIERS glanced up but none stared as I walked through the campsite. Busy with battle preparations, my presence did not concern them. Holding the banner at my side, I looked forward so as not to draw attention to myself. Many sat around the campfire, sharpening pikes and bayonets and loading firearms. All shared a mood of excitement.

Moving around the wall of gabions, I stood over the trench and looked down. A cannon at the end of the trench pointed at the curtain wall. The enemy was in position to attack this very night. My breath froze in my chest.

A soldier walked up behind me. Staring straight ahead, I prayed he would not notice my presence. He spoke in English. I turned slowly around, not knowing if he spoke to me or someone else. He looked directly at me, waiting.

Then he pushed a lit linstock in my hand and nodded toward the cannon at the end of the trench. I stared at the smoldering tip. His eyebrows rose. Knowing that he wanted me to take the linstock to the men waiting by the cannon, I jumped into the trench and feigned walking in that direction. He gestured for me to move with more haste.

I looked away. If I tried to run, the enemy would know of my betrayal. If I handed the linstock to the soldiers waiting by the cannon, I would aid the enemy in breaching the Castillo's walls. If I did nothing, it would alert the enemy to my loyalties. My throat tightened.

Turning away from the soldier, I desperately blew on the linstock. To my despair, the force of my breath increased the redness of the burning hot tip. Pulling it away from my body, I prayed the cold breeze would snuff the life from it, but the glowing linstock grew stronger in the wind. Head held high, I journeyed some distance up the trench where I pretended to fall. Praying the soldier could not see me rub the smoldering tip into the dirt, I ground it as hard as I could until the red went out.

When I turned to check the location of my observer, he was gone. I drew in a long hard breath and thanked the heavens above.

Holding the banner above my head, I slipped out of the trench and walked through the campsite with great urgency, unsure of how long it would take the enemy to learn of my treachery. All around me, soldiers gathered for the attack. They looked past me, unsuspecting.

Looking down so they could not see the panic in my eyes, I thought only of getting back to the Castillo to warn the garrison. The attack would hit my family's side of the courtyard first, where my mother and Grandmamma waited for my return. Thinking of them made my chest grew tight and my breath faint.

Placing my hands on my knees, I breathed slowly in and out trying to catch my breath. Humming filled my ears. I stared down at the ground trying not to lose consciousness. The noise level around me grew as the soldiers' excitement rose. Men carrying flintlocks and pikes ran past on their way toward the trenches. I turned toward the garrison standing along the Castillo's battlements, knowing they did not have enough gunpowder or cannon shot to stop an attack. They could only watch with heavy hearts.

Behind me, a small group of men directed a horse pulling a wagon full of budge barrels toward the tree line. The leader did not care that I stood in the way. He knocked me over without warning and kept going. I fell face down. Those around me did not flinch.

The wagon moved toward a break in the trees, where the soldiers parked it inside a tall group of cedar trees. A second wagon carrying cannonballs and round shot pulled alongside it. A soldier unhitched the second wagon's horse and rode away toward the campsites. All but three of the soldiers followed him on foot.

I stumbled to my feet and pursued them into the trees. Sitting in front of me, in full sight was the enemy's powder magazine. My eyes stared in disbelief as I surveyed my surrounding. The heart of the enemy's power was within my reach. Excitement filled my veins. Biting anxiously on my lower lip, I stole into a nearby thicket of trees to hide.

The three soldiers leaned lazily against the wagon and faced the Castillo. One of them pulled a flask from his jacket and passed it to the others. Each took a long swig before passing it back and forth to each other. Once the first flask was empty, another soldier pulled a second one out. They drank until it too was gone. It was not long before they spoke with slurred words.

I did not know if others would join them or how long only three soldiers would guard the powder magazine, but I thought back to Miguel and his skill with the slingshot and how this would be easy for him. I looked at the Castillo. Miguel's life depended on me. My family depended on me. The garrison depended on me. Every single person depended on me. The consequences of what I was about to do mattered not. All would perish if I did not try.

Stooping down, I picked up two extra-large sweetgum balls with long, prickly spikes and moved cautiously toward the horse. The men facing the Castillo snickered and laughed, unaware of my presence.

I patted the horse lightly on the head and scratched behind its ears. Its tail swished as I stroked the side of its neck, gaining its trust. The men pulled out another flask.

Drawing in a long breath of fresh air, I let it out just as slowly, steadying my hands. Pinching my lips tightly together, I gently lifted the corner of the horse's saddle and slid both sweetgum balls underneath. Then, I lowered the saddle on top of the prickly balls and moved away with great haste.

The pointed spikes dug into the horse's back. It began to fidget. Then kick. While it tried frantically to dislodge the irritant from its back, I pulled my fire stones from my pouch and readied my axe. The men turned around but could not see what troubled the horse.

One of the men got up and stumbled toward the animal. In his clumsiness he fell against the saddle, digging the spikes further into the horse's back. The horse reared up on its hind legs and snapped the wagon posts in two. The heavy wagon flipped over sideways and the horse bolted away, dragging pieces of the wagon tongue behind it.

Barrels of gunpowder crashed to the ground, the wooden staves cracking on impact. Gunpowder poured from the sides. The force knocked the men over. Two of them struggled to stand. They tripped over each other chasing after the horse. The third lay sprawled across the ground not moving. I stared at the heaps of piled gunpowder exposed to the air. If the black powder was damp, my task would be all the more difficult.

Stepping away from the trees, I readied my fire stones, my heart thundering inside my chest. I swallowed the lump in my throat and brought my hand up ready to strike the stones together.

But before I could bring the stones together, an arm jerked me backwards and the fire stones flew into the air and bounced to the ground out of sight. An unknown soldier wrapped his arms around my middle and pinned my arms at my side. As much as I tried, I could not twist my arms free. I stomped on the inside of his foot but he did not lessen his grip. I thrashed wildly back and forth, kicking and jerking with all my strength, but he held tight.

The soldier who had seemed unconscious stumbled to his feet in front of me. Once his hazy eyes focused on our struggle, he pulled a wobbly pistol from his side and pointed it at me. His shaky hand aimed at my heart.

Then I heard a swoosh.

An arrow hit the man in the chest and the pistol dropped from his fingers. He fell over backwards. My captor struggled to retain his balance when someone attacked him from behind. It was then that I took advantage of the chaos and sank my teeth into his hand. He went for my eyes but I bit the fleshy part of the skin between his thumb and finger. He screamed and let go. I spit the blood from my lips.

The man spun around just as Cousin Nico jumped on his back. The force sent Nico flying through the air. Digging my feet into the ground, I rammed into him with my shoulder. Nico stuck his leg out and the man fell over backwards, screaming. I rushed to cover his mouth, but he snapped his teeth at my fingers. Nico kicked the man in the side. The soldier curled into a ball. I reached down, grabbed the knife from my shoe, and held it to his chest. He did not move.

"Nico! Tie his hands behind his back with your belt," I ordered. "Then find two strong vines. We must secure his hands and tie his mouth shut."

"He is the enemy, Pedro. Kill him." Nico gasped for breath.

"No. We take him back to the governor for questioning." I ripped a piece of cloth from my tunic with my free hand and shoved it in the man's mouth. "Hurry before others join him."

Nico did not agree, but he did what I asked. Within moments, he came back with two long, woody vines. We wrapped the longest vine around the prisoner's wrist so many times he could not twist his fingers. Then we secured the cloth inside his mouth by tying the second vine around his head. Pulling another vine from the ground, I wrapped it loosely around the man's legs so he could walk but not run. We did not want to hinder him from moving to the fort.

Nico pointed his dagger toward the Castillo, showing the prisoner the direction. I passed the sack full of herbs and canteens to my cousin.

Picking my bow up off the ground, I removed an arrow from the quiver and looked toward the broken wagon. "Now go. My work here is not finished."

Then Nico did something to surprise me that day: he smirked and punched me in the side. "I will await your return, little cousin. *Vaya con Diós.*"

Pushing the prisoner quickly through the underbrush and toward the fort, it wasn't long before Nico and the prisoner disappeared from sight. Gunfire broke out in the distance. Fearing it was soldiers moving toward the powder magazine, I replaced the arrow in my quiver and moved quickly to locate my fire stones.

Sliding my hands under the ground cover, I sifted through the pine needles and dried leaves trying to find anything that resembled a rough piece of flint and a flat shaft of steel. When I did not find them, I expanded my search to an area outside of where we fought. Both had landed inside a tangle of tree roots.

I placed the fire stones back inside my pouch and looked up. That is when I saw two soldiers rushing across open ground toward me, their lanterns swaying rapidly back and forth. I slipped behind the trees and over the underbrush toward a group of tree trunks. Crawling swiftly on hands and knees, I passed the trunks of many trees before finding one with low hanging tree branches. I pulled myself up out of sight.

The soldiers walked slowly across the ground searching for my tracks, but as fortune would have it, my footprints blended in with the many made earlier in the day. They passed directly under my nose. I could have reached down and plucked a hair from one of their heads. My racing heart pounded with such force, I feared they would hear it. Drawing in a long slow breath, I held it for fear of discovery.

Gunfire erupted near the trenches. The soldiers turned and doubled back toward the broken wagon.

I slipped out of the tree and looked around. The area was clear. After scooping up a handful of Spanish moss and removing a small container full of pig fat from the bottom of my quiver, I placed the strongest arrow between my knees. My hands trembled as I tore cloth from my sleeve, wrapped it with dry moss into a tight ball around the shaft just below the arrowhead, coated it in pig fat, and secured it in place with a short piece of dried vine.

Then the sound of crunching leaves crackled in the distance. The sight of two more enemy soldiers appeared at the broken wagon. Slipping behind the tree trunks once again, I prayed enemy eyes had not fallen on me.

Now a party of four, the soldiers moved cautiously around the wagon studying the destruction and nearby tracks. One of them singled out my footprints. Another spotted the tracks made by Nico and the prisoner. They fanned out in different directions, their paths closing in around me from all sides. I recognized the pattern all too well as a tactic used by hunters to enclose a trapped animal. In the distance, another set of soldiers ran toward me, their swaying lanterns making streaks of light across the horizon.

Fear surged up my spine, but I could not yield to the feeling. I moved out in the open to where I had a clear shot of the wagon. Holding the arrow between my knees, I faced the tip out, felt inside my small pouch, and pulled the fire stones out. When I struck the steel against the edge of the flint, they hit with such force, an umbrella of hot sparks showered the moss. A small tuft of smoke appeared, then the moss ignited into a flaming ball of fire.

The soldiers shouted directions to each other. I slipped the arrow into the bow and aimed at the pile of broken budge barrels. The arrow went straight. A flintlock fired. A sharp, hot stab entered my side. The ground came up to meet me.

Then an enormous ball of flames exploded in the night sky, setting the trees around it on fire. The earth-shattering explosion that followed sent reverberations rolling across the ground beneath me and I fell unconscious.

35

Grandpapa

Surviving spies, finally, are those who bring back news from the enemy's camp.— Sun Tzu

I DO NOT KNOW HOW LONG I was unconscious, nor was I witness to what happened next. Juan Felipe and Nico saw the destruction from the battlements. The enemy was in such disarray that they did not concern themselves with my seemingly lifeless body some distance from the accident.

Pandemonium broke out. The soldiers who were not injured struggled to contain the damage. The blast had also destroyed the second wagon full of supplies and set the trees ablaze. The wind carried the flames from the trees to the nearby tents. Fire jumped from tent to tent as soldiers hurried to subdue the crisis.

Juan Felipe and Nico entered the woods and waited until enemy eyes were busy elsewhere to pull me from the site. They dragged me through the woods, across the marsh, and into the moat, where the garrison helped lift my lifeless form up the curtain wall with ropes.

***

DECEMBER 24TH

The air was crisp, the blue sky clear and the sun bright. Two days and nights had passed by the time I awoke to find a blanket tucked around my neck and Grandmamma leaning over me with a poultice of herbs. An excruciating pain radiated from my side, a ringing in my ears throbbed, and I could not lift my head.

"You are fortunate to be with us, grandson," said Grandmamma stroking my forehead. "How do you fare?"

I blinked, trying to clear my eyes. "I cannot feel my right leg and my ears feel as if they are stuffed with cloth."

She lifted the blanket and pushed on my wound. I winced.

Her brows wrinkled when she lowered the blanket back in place. "Your ears will recover from the blast with time and the redness in your wound grows less. It will be up to the Almighty whether you regain the use of your right leg. The surgeon and I have removed the musket ball and cauterized the wound in your back, being careful to remove all the pieces of cloth that tore from your tunics and lodged inside the wound. It was fortunate that you wore so many layers. Those layers of clothing stopped the bullet from reaching your spine. The wound will leave an unsightly scar but your grandpapa would have proudly called this a *wound of honor.*" She handed me a wooden bowl full of broth. "Now drink this."

I did not take the bowl from her hands but stared into her eyes instead. "Grandpapa *would have* called it a wound of honor? What has happened that you speak these words?"

She looked down, her red rimmed eyes filling with tears. "I am sorry to burden you with sad news at such a time, but your grandpapa has left us, Pedro. Our Lord in Heaven has called him home. His suffering is over."

I closed my eyes and swallowed. Every muscle in my body ached and my side was so tender I was afraid to breathe. My head throbbed and my throat felt as if it was covered in blisters, but those things were nothing compared to the dagger lodged inside my heart. "I was not prepared for him to go. We still fight the enemy. He said he would be here."

If Grandmamma said more, I did not hear her words, nor did I care. I curled into a ball. A knot formed in my throat. My eyes became blurry and my chest became heavy. I turned away, my lips pressed tightly together. An enormous weight strangled my insides.

I thought back to when Grandpapa taught me to how to fish. We sat in the canoe in the middle of the river for hours waiting for the fish to bite. I wanted to speak, but he would press his finger to his lips, point to the fish, and shake his head. I did not like to be silent for so long, but we would happily return with a basket full of fish.

It was he who taught me how to use a hammerstone to chip away a piece of flint until it took the shape of an arrowhead. He was the one who taught me how to weave a funnel-shaped weir to trap ducks and how to judge the distance of my prey by looking down the barrel of a musket. He showed me which branches make the best bows by bending them on the tree first and how to fashion arrows that fly true. He taught me how to whittle the roughest piece of wood into a fine figure and how to steady my hand so I could throw a knife with perfect accuracy.

Tears fell from my cheeks. I lay still for a long time, not speaking to anyone. My thoughts did not turn to Miguel, nor did I inquire about the enemy. The only thing breaking the silence around me were the irritable voices of the crowd carrying across the courtyard and laughing seagulls circling overhead. I swallowed, lost in my memories.

Whispering softly to myself, I spoke the words troubling my heart. "Grandpapa, you taught me that a wise person judges others more by their actions and less by their words. I will remember those words always. But you also told me to stand tall and hold my chin up no matter my destiny. But I cannot stand tall, Grandpapa. I don't know how. I have failed."

My chest heaved up and down. Resting my head against my arms, my sleeves became heavy with tears.

Uncle Manuel knelt beside my bed and stroked my back. I did not look at his eyes.

"I miss Grandpapa, too," he said. "He lives inside us. We will never forget him."

I turned away so he could not see my face twisted in grief.

He turned toward Grandmamma. "It has been confirmed by the prisoner Nico and Pedro captured that the enemy's gunpowder is very low and the soldiers are unhappy. Many of the soldiers speak of leaving. Last night's assault on the Castillo was to be a major victory for the enemy and now, that victory has failed. If the Castillo is able to stay strong, the enemy may tire of this fight and leave. We have proven to be much stronger than they anticipated."

Grandmamma pulled the covers up around my shoulders.

Uncle Manuel sighed. "Pedro's brave deed has proven to me that he is my brother's son many times, but we do not know how long this reprieve will last. The enemy waits for reinforcements and bombs from Jamaica just as we wait for reinforcements from Cuba. I do not think they are able to continue their assault on the Castillo's walls, but we cannot rely on this. If this were to happen, we have only a little gunpowder and the use of our swords, machetes, and pikes against an army of more than a thousand."

Grandmamma tucked the edges of the blanket into my collar. I reached up and pulled it out. Smiling gently to herself, she patted me affectionately on the arm and left the blanket where it lay. Uncle Manuel stood and pulled Grandmamma to the side, away from where I lay.

"Mother, how is Pedro? Should I worry about my brother's son?"

"Pedro will survive if the town survives the siege. When you are in the chapel, pray the Almighty gives him the use of his right leg. Right now his spirit suffers, as do ours, with the passing of his grandpapa. This does not help. A person's spirit must be strong in order to heal the body, but his spirit suffers greatly." Her voice quavered.

Uncle Manuel's voice grew small. "I understand this all too well, Mother. My own heart suffers because of father's passing, but I do not have time to grieve. Father ordered me to defeat the enemy. I do this for the Crown and for the family, but I also do this for him. His voice lives inside my heart and he would expect us to carry on."

Grandmamma struggled to speak. "You are his son, Manuel. He would expect no less of you. You are the man he raised you to be and he was very proud of you."

They became quiet. I swallowed, my tears threatening to choke me. My chest heaved. I wanted Grandmamma and my uncle to go away. I did not want to hear about the war or the pride Grandpapa held for Uncle Manuel. Despite my wishes to be alone, they remained.

It wasn't long before Nico arrived, out of breath. Pushing against the bottom of my bedding with my good leg, I rolled over, away from the family so I would not have to see my cousin's face.

"Papa . . . I came as fast as I could," said Nico. "I have news from the garrison and I must also speak with Pedro."

"What news does the garrison send?" Uncle Manuel asked.

Nico drew in a deep breath. "Two ships . . . have been spotted on the horizon."

My uncle's voice grew stern. "Friend or foe?"

"The governor is hopeful that the ships are Spanish."

Uncle Manuel ground his fist into the palm of his open hand. "Let us pray the governor is right."

Sighing quietly to myself, I did not share the governor's optimism. If they were Spanish, how would they pass the many English ships guarding the fort? They would be greatly outnumbered and outgunned. And if the ships were English, that meant reinforcements had arrived. That also meant the enemy would be in position to storm the Castillo's wall this very night, if they so chose. I swallowed.

Grandmamma whispered. "And if they are English, Manuel? Does the governor understand how weary the people grow? They fear for their lives night and day. They forget themselves. Tempers flare over matters of no importance. Their words are full of hate. They fight over who uses the cooking pot. They fight over who goes to the chapel. They fight over the latrines. They fight over how much water a family drinks. They fight over rations of food. Many are restless and cannot sleep. Families and friends of many years have become bitter enemies."

"The governor is aware of this, Mother, and it concerns him both night and day," said Uncle Manuel gravely. "Now, tell us, Nico, what news do you have for Pedro?"

"The priest has just given last rites to Carlos Fernando and he has confessed to his sins. The whole family must hear what I have to report on Pedro's father."

I sat up. My wounds gave me pause, but I did not give in to the pain. It was important I hear every word. "What did that viper Carlos Fernando say, Nico?"

Nico knelt beside me. "I am sorry for everything I have said and done to you, little cousin. You did not deserve it. I have been a fool to listen to such lies."

I cared only about the words Nico held back. "Pray tell, what sins did Carlos Fernando confess?"

He looked at me with eyes full of regret. "It was Carlos Fernando who was the spy, not your father. He was the one who gave our secrets to the enemy a long time ago. When your father realized what Carlos was doing, he followed him into the enemy campsite to keep Carlos from sharing our secrets. But the enemy caught your father and killed him. Carlos told everyone your father was the spy so they would not suspect him."

I straightened my shoulders, ignoring the sharp stabbing pains gripping my side. "I knew my father had not acted against the Crown or his family. His soul could not have possessed such evil." My heart raced inside my chest.

"There is more, little cousin," said Nico. "Carlos confessed to the priest that when your father sacrificed his life to protect the town, it filled him with remorse. Because of your father's sacrifice, Carlos did not work as a spy after that. He has carried this burden with a heavy heart ever since and prays that you understand that he was a coward and was ashamed and he did not have the courage to confess this sooner."

Grandmamma lowered her head, her eyes filled with tears. Uncle Manuel wrapped his arms around her. She sobbed while he rocked her back and forth. I looked down, my chin trembling.

Uncle Manuel turned his eyes on me. "Your grandpapa did not want you to hear such tales and forbade us from telling you. He did not want you to grow up under such a dark shadow and he did not want to give life to rumors that held no truth. Many knew your father well and did not believe such nonsense. We will set the record straight, Pedro. Do not concern yourself with that."

I nodded, knowing that my father had died a patriot and not a coward or a traitor. I breathed a little easier. Gone was the emptiness that has plagued me since I was a little boy. Gone was the angst of not knowing why some had shunned me. Hearing Carlos Fernando's words had soothed a part of my troubled heart. I rubbed my chest. But it did not erase the hole left by Grandpapa's passing.

Grandmamma dried her tears, and looking lovingly up at Uncle Manuel, patted him softly on the chest before stepping away. He smiled at her.

I struggled to sit up. "How is Miguel?" I asked.

Wiping her eyes one last time, Grandmamma picked up the bowl of broth she had offered me earlier and held it to my mouth. This time I drank from it.

"Our prayers have been answered," she said. "His wound has closed and he has lost weight but he is still with us. Your mother takes good care of him. When I am there, he asks about you and I have told him all that has happened. He only regrets that he was not there with you."

I wiped the bitter broth from my lips. "I will pray for his fast recovery."

"Miguel is fortunate to have a friend such as you," said Uncle Manuel. "Without you to gather the medicine your grandmamma needed, he and others would not . . ."

"Yes, yes, Miguel and Pedro are good friends," said Nico interrupting. "But without me, my little cousin would be worm food. I risked my own life to save him from the enemy and pull him back to the Castillo."

I turned toward Nico, unable to suppress a tight smile. "You owe me, Nico. I will take your actions in the woods as a small payment for the years of misery you have caused me."

Nico pulled back, his brows raised in surprise. He started to say something but thought better of it and closed his mouth instead. Laughing, Uncle Manuel patted us both on the head.

It was then that another member of the garrison arrived with a message. The messenger pulled Uncle Manuel aside and whispered in his ear. When the messenger had finished, Uncle Manuel grabbed Nico by the arm and the three of them left without saying a word.

36

Anastasia Island

*According as circumstances are favorable,
one should modify one's plans.* — Sun Tzu

"THE SHIPS ARE ENGLISH!" cried the guard from the lookout tower.

Clutching my arms to my chest, I shifted uneasily in my bed. People panicked all around me. Women whimpered and children cried. People rushed to the chapel where the small room could not accommodate such numbers. The garrison fired a shot across the harbor.

Uncle Manuel left the governor's counsel, walked briskly to the middle of the courtyard, and addressed the crowd. "The governor bids you to stay calm. He remains hopeful that help approaches from Cuba. Find solace in knowing that we have survived a two-month siege from a superior army and we will continue to do so."

The crowd murmured. Many remained fretful.

"The governor seeks to reward the garrison," he continued, "for their tireless efforts to defend the Castillo and has ordered bonuses for them. And he invites everyone to join him this evening in celebrating Christmas Eve. The garrison will be issuing extra food rations and the governor has ordered the pigs slaughtered for a feast. The priests are preparing for a midnight mass."

The thought of extra food and festivities softened the crowd's mood.

Grandmamma pulled Uncle Manuel to the side. "This is well and good, Manuel, and these actions may lift the spirits of some, but how can the governor order bonuses for the garrison? We do not have the money. This is a desperate move to disguise our true fate. Many will see through this."

There was no hint of deceit in Uncle Manuel's voice. "Mama, the governor remains optimistic. He knows the morale of the garrison is low and that people must remain hopeful or they will not survive. The garrison cannot think all is lost. Men who have lost hope do not fight with conviction."

She stared into his eyes, reading his thoughts for a long time. "Then it is our duty to be thankful. Your father would have bid me to help in the celebrations, so this I will do." She patted his cheek.

Uncle Manuel bid us farewell and left to organize the celebrations. It wasn't long before the garrison began passing out wine and extra rations of food. Within hours, the smell of roasting pork filled the air.

Grandmamma busied herself stirring a small pot of plum pudding over the fire. The amount of milk that she was able to obtain was small, but it was enough for the few plums she had saved for the occasion. She cooked Grandpapa's favorite Christmas pudding, a tradition she had started when they first married. We always laughed, knowing he wouldn't share one spoonful with the rest of us. This time, when the pain of losing him came, I inhaled and let it slowly out.

The winter sun set early, painting a night sky filled with stars and a half moon. Light from the lanterns and many candles brought the courtyard to life. A familiar silhouette made its way through the candlelight and hobbled toward me. Miguel's younger brother and sister supported him as he used his quarter-pike as a crutch.

He called out from the crowd. "I would have come sooner, but my mother would not let me leave. It wasn't until your uncle arrived that she listened."

When he came closer, it was then that I saw the hollowness of his face and how his eyes had sunk into it. "It is good that you are alive, my friend," I replied. "Did my uncle bring news of your father?"

Stepping around a small group of children practicing their Christmas play, he and his siblings moved slowly through a crowd busy with festival preparations. "According to the messenger, my father and the others are well, but unable to send help. They fight to keep the enemy from spreading. Every time my mother hears that my father is well, she weeps with joy."

When he finally reached my side, I grabbed him by the shoulders and hugged him as never before. His brother and sister left to join their family in the festivities.

Miguel looked down, patting me feebly on the shoulder. "Pedro, I came to tell you how sorry I am to hear about your grandpapa. I will miss him greatly."

I nodded. We looked at each other, not saying a word. We did not need to.

Then he hobbled over to the top of the trunk and sat down. "Look at us now. Ranson would call us two wounded birds."

My side throbbed and my bad leg felt weak but I did not say so. "I wonder how that scoundrel fares. At least he is free to make his own decisions and go where he chooses. It vexes me that I am trapped inside this fort and cannot fight. I keep my bow and axe ready at my side."

Miguel laid his quarter-pike on the ground. "We are cripples, Pedro. We cannot defend ourselves against a group of little boys, let alone stop the English from getting reinforcements."

I crossed my arms. "Speak for yourself, Miguel. As long as my body draws breath, I will never give up."

He punched me lightly in the chest. "I expect no less."

I pretended to punch him back.

Despite our aches and pains, we laughed. We boasted of our adventures, recalling our fire canoes, his first time hunting gopher turtle, and how the enemy captured me when I dropped out of a tree in front of them. We laughed about our adventure inside a trunk smelling of alligator and how we managed to swallow half an oyster bed in one meal. He reminded me of our capture by the Yamasee Indians and I reminded him about the scout and his father's canteen. When we had laughed long enough, and felt whole again, we sat for a long time just staring at the beautiful night sky.

A harp and *vihuelas* filled the Castillo with music. Many in the crowd danced while a group of boys challenged each other to a bullfight. Nico, playing the bull, cupped his hands over his head and charged. The boys dodged his attacks and pretended to spear him with sticks. The bull grabbed his sides, pretended to wail in pain, and rolled over dead. The crowd laughed and had a merry time.

At midnight the priests performed the mass under the twinkling black sky. For a few treasured hours, the townspeople felt like families and friends again. When the last candle went out for the night, Christmas Day had arrived and the Castillo still stood.

37

Uncle Manuel

Move not unless you see an advantage; use not your troops unless there is something to be gained; fight not unless the position is critical. — Sun Tzu

I AWOKE EARLY CHRISTMAS MORNING to a bright morning sun rising over the horizon. My back ached and it hurt to move my leg but some of the feeling had come back. A strength that I had not felt in a long time had returned. I stretched and sat up.

Many walked through the campsite toward the small chapel. Members of the garrison moved silently through the crowd. Nico joined the others in their duties but none spoke. They filled water jugs from the well, manned the ramp to the gun deck, passed out food rations, and kept order at the latrines.

Able to stand for a brief amount of time, I picked up the empty water jug and edged slowly to the water well, where I waited in line for Juan Felipe to pass out the rations. When it was my turn, I placed my jug on the ground while he pulled the water up from the shaft.

"What news do you have for me today?" I asked.

"I cannot say," he answered with pinched eyebrows.

I looked at him. "Pray tell, why not?"

"The governor has forbidden the garrison from speaking."

I narrowed my eyes. "It is me, Pedro. If Grandpapa were alive, he would trust me with the garrison's news."

"But he is not here to tell you, Pedro. I suggest you ask your uncle if you seek to know more. If I talk, I will be charged a penalty."

He poured water into my jug and pushed it toward me. I squatted, held the jug close to my chest, and pulled myself slowly up. Confused by Juan Felipe's reluctance to speak, I labored to get across the courtyard to the family campsite, where I lowered the heavy jug slowly to the ground.

The relief I felt at sitting once again was enormous. One little task had left me exhausted. I turned toward Grandmamma and watched as she made our allotment of flour into dough. "I did not know such a small jug of water could be so heavy. When is Uncle Manuel coming?"

She did not look up. "Once your strength has returned, you will be as before, but until then, you move only when necessary. I am able to carry the water, Pedro. Please rest."

I stared, waiting for her to answer.

Setting her dough to the side, she glanced up before transferring the water from the jug to her cooking pot. "Uncle Manuel will come when he is able."

"I need to speak to him. Something important has happened and Juan Felipe refuses to confide in me."

She dug a clove of garlic from her pouch and sliced it into small slices. "The two English ships, a brigantine and a sloop, have put down anchors at Anastasia Island."

"What?" I pulled my axe out from under my blankets. "Then do not look for me. I am going up to the gun deck to speak with Uncle Manuel. There must be something I am able to do."

Grandmamma set her cooking pot down. "Pedro, you are barely able to stand. Your leg drags behind you and there is nothing for you to do. You will only be in the way. It is more important that you rest or you will not heal properly."

"Put a new poultice on my wound or give me your broth to drink, but I must take my leave. I will not rest until I do."

Sighing softly to herself, Grandmamma changed the poultice around my wound and bid me to drink an extra-large bowl of bitter willow bark tea. As soon as I had drunk the last drop, I wiped my mouth across my sleeve, walked slowly past the family campsites to the bottom of the ramp, and looked up. The ramp was not so long, but it would prove to be difficult to climb nevertheless.

Nico stood guard at the bottom. To my surprise, he stepped back and let me pass. "You look better today, little cousin. The color has returned to your ugly face," he grinned.

I was too weary to trade insults with him. "What happens that the governor forbids the garrison from speaking?"

"I cannot say, but my father has given you permission to be on the gun deck."

Without saying more, I pushed him out of the way and started slowly up the ramp to the top. Despite my cousin's civility, I could not stop the anger toward him for his past actions from rising up inside me. Perhaps in time my dislike would lessen. My uncle watched the ships through a field glass. A group of artillerymen prepared the cannons behind us.

Moving closer, I leaned against the wall next to him. "Does the enemy unload reinforcements?"

He did not look up from studying the island. "The sloop's ramp is down but we cannot see beyond that. We must plan for the worst and assume she unloads ammunition. The sloop is not within reach of our cannons but we prepare for the opportunity. I have ordered a group of men to storm the island and destroy their supplies."

I drew back. "But any soldier leaving the protection of the fort will be killed. The enemy surrounds us on every side. If our soldiers use boats to cross to the island, they will be within range of English weapons."

Uncle Manuel did not say more. It became clear as to why the soldiers were forbidden to speak. The garrison could not wait until sunset because it would give the enemy time to unload and distribute their ammunition, if they did indeed possess such cargo. The only hope of outlasting the enemy was for some of our men to survive long enough to destroy the enemy's supplies. Sending a group of men to the island was to ask them to sacrifice their lives.

I shook my head. "No, Uncle, let me go. I will lie flat against the bottom of a canoe. If the canoe appears empty and drifts along the water without direction, the enemy will think it abandoned. Then I will set my arrows ablaze and fire on them with my bow. I do not need the use of my legs for such a task. I can do this, Uncle."

Uncle Manuel looked at me, neither amusement nor sadness filling his eyes. "Pedro, you are injured and I cannot trust something so important to a boy, although your heart is in the right place. I will be leading a group of volunteers as soon as preparations are complete."

I stumbled back in surprise. "You? But you cannot go! You will die. Who will lead the troops?"

He looked me in the eyes. "If I do not do this, there will be no troops to lead. There will be no fort to protect. You and everyone I love will fall to the enemy. I would not be able to live with myself if I did not do everything possible that I know to do. It is as it should be, Pedro. This is what is required of me."

Losing Grandpapa had been hard enough, but losing my uncle was not something I had considered. A knot formed in my throat. I struggled to find words to say but could find none. As much as I did not want him to go, I admired his decision.

Miguel, leaning on his quarter-pike, walked slowly up the ramp and stood next to me. We nodded to each other.

Uncle Manuel handed the field glass to me. "You and Miguel may observe what takes place. It is time I go, Pedro. I must say goodbye to my family and your grandmamma before departing."

I passed the field glass to Miguel and informed him of the events to come.

He studied the island. "There is nothing we can do, Pedro, but pray."

We saw the garrison, holding bundles of clothes and dragging an English prisoner behind them, enter the moat below. Uncle Manuel took off his jacket and his trousers and dropped any items belonging to his uniform on the ground. The garrison did the same. Then they picked up clothes commonly worn by prisoners and put them on. Sliding pistols under their tunics, they stooped to hide knives inside their shoes. An English prisoner, now wearing Uncle Manuel's Spanish uniform, fidgeted nervously in place while a guard kept watch.

"Clever. Uncle Manuel seeks to confuse the enemy. The garrison is dressed as English prisoners and the English prisoner is dressed to look like a Spanish officer."

Miguel frowned. "Do you think this will deceive the enemy?"

I sighed. "Let us pray that the enemy thinks the governor is trying to negotiate a surrender by releasing a party of English prisoners in good faith."

English soldiers occupying the town guarded the Matanzas River with flintlocks. English soldiers on the island guarded the sloop and its bounty. The ability to fire at the longboats from both sides of the river posed a problem for the garrison. Once the enemy caught sight of the longboats, the garrison wouldn't have a prayer of surviving. My chest felt hollow inside.

The garrison readied the boats. They launched from the bank directly in front of the east wall and rowed steadily out into the river. The prisoner dressed as an officer stood at the front of the first longboat. He pointed toward the island like he commanded the others. A pistol pointed at his head rested just beneath the rim of the boat where no eyes could see.

Not far from the fort, enemy soldiers on both sides of the river came out of hiding. They moved closer to the shore where they watched the longboats row toward the island. The *capitán* of the sloop left the site where his men unloaded supplies and walked toward the soldiers gathered on the beach. He held a field glass to his eye and watched the approaching longboats.

The deception appeared as it should. The garrison dressed as prisoners looked down, rowing steadily across the water toward the island. The prisoner dressed as a commander stood straight, his head held high, with his arm outstretched pointing the way.

I do not know what went wrong after that. Perhaps the pistol aimed at the prisoner's chest rose above the rim of the boat, or the garrison was not convincing in their duties, or perhaps the English *capitán* from the sloop recognized the prisoner posing as an officer, but the deception ended too soon.

The *capitán* gave an order. The soldier next to him pulled his flintlock up to his shoulder, aimed, and fired. CRACK! The shot smacked the water in front of the hull. Within seconds, the enemy on both sides of the river moved into position and opened fire. To avoid a direct hit, the garrison slid underneath the rim of the boats and pulled the oars inside. The prisoner dropped to the bottom of the boat and did not move.

Only a moment passed before the oars reappeared in the water again. To my surprise and great relief, the garrison reversed course and headed back toward the Castillo. The Castillo's musketeers shot from the gun deck. A cannon took aim at the island. BOOM! A fire fight broke out between the Castillo and the English soldiers. An exchange of force erupted on both sides of the river until the garrison was safely inside the Castillo.

38

December 26, 1702

Do not swallow bait offered by the enemy. Do not interfere with an army that is returning home. — Sun Tzu

UNCLE MANUEL SAT ON THE TRUNK gritting his teeth while Grandmamma cleaned and treated his wounds.

"I must be sure your wounds are clean or they will fester, Manuel. We are fortunate that the sun was in the enemy's eyes yesterday or the garrisons' wounds would be more severe. It was wise to return to the Castillo when you did. Our soldiers would not have reached the sloop alive. Providence protected you." Blood ran down Uncle Manuel's arm while she tugged on the gaping wound at the top. He bit his lip, wincing. "Hush," she scolded. "You whimper like a small child."

Despite the grim circumstances we now suffered inside the fort, I laughed. That was a mistake.

Uncle Manuel's face tightened in pain but his eyes found me. "You are forbidden from talking about this, Pedro." Then he looked back at Grandmamma. "It was my duty to try, Mother. But we exhausted our remaining ammunition. Now we are completely defenseless."

Grandmamma prodded the wound again before pouring her special blend of warm tannin water and herbs into his wound. She dried the affected area with a clean cloth before stretching the skin with her fingers. He stared at the ground, his lips pressed tightly together in silence.

"The decision was wise, Manuel. Do not doubt yourself. Your father would have said the same. I must use thorns to hold the wound closed," she said while pinching the flesh shut. "Hold still while I weave the injured skin together and secure the thorns. The thorns will be easy to dislodge so you must be very mindful of this arm or we will need to open the wound and begin again. The wound was deep but the muscles will heal and you will be as before."

I looked at my shoes, avoiding the sight of Grandmamma's skillful hands pushing the long, pointed thorns through the skin. She had used her thorns on me when I had accidentally sliced into my hand while skinning a deer. I still remember the piercing pain caused by the sharp tips and the tenderness of my wound as she fastened the flesh together. The thought made me shudder. I could not fault my uncle for complaining.

"What will happen next, Uncle?" I said, directing my eyes away.

"We have an advantage that the enemy does not possess," he replied.

I frowned, not sure of his meaning.

"We must weigh only the facts and not what we currently surmise. We are under siege. We do not determine our destiny. Our mission each day is to survive. And each day, we plan our strategies and execute those plans." He stopped to watch Grandmamma secure a bandage over the thorns and wound. She placed a poultice over the wounded skin before securing the cloth around his arm.

"I do not see that as an advantage," I said.

He looked up. "It is an advantage because we know what we must do. We live each day knowing that we cannot deviate from our path. But our enemy has choices. They sleep in the cold, live away from their warm homes and their families. They are hungry and discontent. Many came for the glory and for the riches. They have found very little of both. An easy victory slipped away from them when Governor Zúñiga received advance warning of their initial attack from the Chacato woman. We have intercepted their spies. They have been unable to stop our messengers from leaving the fort and our coquina walls absorbed their cannonballs, making their artillery ineffective. We were able to drive cattle into our moat, giving us food to survive. They did not receive the reinforcements they needed to overwhelm us. A few of the enemy have already returned to their former lives." He stopped and frowned.

"But if the sloop carries ammunition," I said, "our destiny has now changed."

Nodding reluctantly in agreement, he struggled to slip his tunic over his wound using only one arm. Grandmamma fussed about his uniform placing too much pressure on his injury. After a lengthy debate between the two of them, Uncle Manuel relented and agreed to wear a sling.

That was when a member of the garrison appeared at our campsite to request an audience with my uncle. Lowering his head and moving closer to Uncle Manuel, the messenger kept his voice low. "Governor Moore has sent a messenger."

Uncle Manuel straightened. "And the message?"

"The governor urgently requests you join him in his chambers. The enemy has ordered us to surrender in two hours."

Despite my injured ears, each troubling word came out clearly. I choked on the news. For a brief second, silence followed. Then Uncle Manuel bid Grandmamma farewell and pushed past the crowd blocking the courtyard. The messenger followed. They were out of sight before I turned around.

My heart beat rapidly inside my chest. The sloop had carried bombs.

My thoughts turned to Moore's army. Burned homes, destroyed missions, ruined villages, and conquered lands. I thought of stolen treasure and desecrated churches. I thought of devastated farm land and slaughtered animals. And I thought of native Indians loyal to Spain captured and sold as slaves. I thought of those that had lost their lives and the many wounded in their path. The weight of a thousand stones pressed against my heart. It was no wonder I jumped when Miguel stepped in front of me.

"What agitates you so?" he asked.

I pulled him close to me. "Moore has demanded our surrender. The governor has two hours to decide."

Miguel's eyes grew wide. "I do not understand."

I shook my head. "We are trapped inside these walls. We cannot see beyond the boundaries of the fort. The sloop must have delivered ammunition. Or a ship, one we cannot see, unloaded supplies farther up the beach."

"But why would Moore demand our surrender? Why not breach the walls and take the Castillo? Has he not planned that all along?" he asked.

I hesitated, thinking. "Uncle Manuel says the soldiers grow weary and many desire to return home. Perhaps they weary of the battle." I looked away, not really believing this to be the reason. "But, a few days ago, I saw soldiers anxious to breach the walls. I do not trust this. Something is wrong."

Miguel and I made our way to the gun deck. Nico patted my shoulder when I passed and I nodded at him. Knowing Grandpapa would have approved of that small action soothed my heart. Enemy ships sat in the same positions as the day before, anchored out of cannon range. We saw no activity on board or any indications of preparing for an attack.

Miguel and I returned to where Nico stood guard on the eastern wall. "Can you tell me, cousin, what news comes from the surrender?"

Nico said nothing.

"May I remind you, cousin, that you owe me?"

Nico looked toward the courtyard before reluctantly answering. "Moore will let the people go in exchange for Governor Zúñiga, his officers, and the Castillo. The fort must remain unharmed, complete with all of its treasure. The people may only take the clothes on their backs, but they will be allowed a safe exit from the territory."

The hairs on the back of my neck bristled. "That means Uncle Manuel would be one of the prisoners. The people are weak, many are wounded, and many would starve before traveling far enough to find shelter. The governor cannot be considering such an offer," I said. "What power does Moore have to make such a request?"

"Moore claims he has received bombs from Jamaica and he has captured the garrison protecting our outlying missions and Apalachee. The English control all of the land outside of the Castillo. We are surrounded by the enemy. If we do not agree to his terms of surrender, he will breach the walls and take every life within it."

I looked at Miguel. He showed no emotion at hearing the news of his father's capture. I wondered if he felt nothing, or he had truly mastered his fear and did not show it.

Miguel spoke in a soft voice. "It is clear Moore wants the Castillo unharmed. He wants it as a trophy."

I nodded. My friend showed wisdom. "The Castillo is the finest fort in La Florida and if the English control it, they control all of La Florida and the Gulf Stream used by the Spanish fleet. It would be a terrible blow to the Crown for the Castillo to fall under enemy hands. They would lose their shipping lanes and foothold in La Florida."

Miguel looked down, this news weighing heavily on his mood.

I calmed my voice but held my head high. "I do not believe the English have captured Apalachee or that they have bombs."

Nico and Miguel stared at me.

"Why do you say this, Pedro?" asked Nico.

"My gut tells me this is a falsehood. It is the same as when I was little and my older brothers and I played war. We would lie and cheat to win. We did not play for honor or glory. We played to win. That was all that mattered. I believe Moore seeks to deceive us because he has nothing to lose and everything to gain. I must speak with the governor."

Miguel narrowed his eyes. "What else does your gut tell you? You have not revealed it all."

I folded my arms. "If the enemy had bombs, there would be excitement in the enemy camp, such as the night I walked among them. I am the only person to have been with the enemy and understand this. When I look at the enemy camp now, it is lifeless and still. How could this be if the enemy received reinforcements?"

"And?" asked Miguel.

"And Uncle Manuel reports some of the enemy has returned to their homes. Why would soldiers spend weeks fighting and then return home before the victory? They would lose any reward they were fighting to win."

"Perhaps it was a falsehood that some of the enemy have returned home," said Miguel. "And reinforcements have only arrived today so they would not have known of this advantage. Perhaps you make your assumptions on something that has not happened."

"No," said Nico. "The garrison has witnessed a small number of the enemy leaving. One of the small ships outside the harbor has departed in the last hour."

Miguel slapped my arm with the back of his hand. "Perhaps it moves to a more strategic position. But I do not think so . . . I believe as you do, Pedro. I have learned to trust your gut."

Nico turned to leave. "I will take your argument before my father so he can present it to the governor."

Filled with concern, Miguel and I passed the hour on the gun deck, watching the garrison clean the cannons, their muskets, and sharpen their knives and bayonets. When a small group of soldiers lowered the Spanish flag from the pole, we demanded to know why the garrison removed such an important symbol of the Spanish Empire.

Juan Felipe folded the flag into a triangle. "The governor has agreed to Moore's terms. He wishes to preserve the people and the garrison captured while protecting the territories. Before this day is done, an English flag will fly over the Castillo."

I swallowed, desperate to think. "This is a mistake. I must speak with the governor. Now."

Juan Felipe shook his head and looked straight ahead. "Mind your manners, Pedro. The governor has listened to your objections and has considered them as well as the opinions of his council. What he does now, he does for the future of the people. We prepare the Castillo for Moore's arrival. Moore will inspect the fort before signing the terms of our surrender. Rest assured, Pedro, Governor Zúñiga does not make this decision lightly. It is with a heavy heart that he succumbs to these terms. You must trust him."

"But the threat from the enemy has no teeth. They seek to deceive us," I argued.

"I said silence, young Pedro. Do not push this further. Your life and that of your family has been spared. Your objections have been voiced and decisions have been made. Now go tell your family so they may prepare to depart."

Juan Felipe tucked the flag under his arm and walked away. Miguel and I stared at each other, our hearts heavy with defeat. The long faces of the garrison followed our movements as we moved slowly down the ramp to the courtyard. A sea of chaos stirred at the bottom of the plank.

39

Surrender

The Commander stands for the virtues of wisdom, sincerity, benevolence, courage and strictness. — Sun Tzu

"EVERYONE WILL BE GIVEN SAFE PASSAGE out of the territory, but you may only take the clothes on your backs and no more. Now go and prepare to leave," announced Juan Felipe in a loud voice.

A frantic crowd rushed to prepare for an exit out of the fort and into hostile territory but the garrison protected the gate. Wails of despair and sobs echoed all around us. People pulled on extra layers of clothing trying to salvage whatever they could from their belongings. Many hid small possessions inside the folds of their tunics and trousers.

I watched the mayhem. Before the siege, I was but a boy. Since then, I had learned what it meant to walk through the fire of battle and come out alive on the other side. I had learned what real hardship was and how life could vanish within the blink of an eye. I had learned what it felt like to be without a home, to be thirsty, to have your stomach gnaw at the back of your spine, and how it felt to be so frightened you cannot move. I knew what it meant to be consumed with worry, to fight all night long in your sleep, and to lose all hope.

I looked down, doubling my fists in anger. This fort had been my home for two months, and a large part of my life since I was born. The Castillo de San Marcos was part of me and if Moore had his way, this would be the last time I stood within her walls.

Grandmamma, grasping Grandpapa's rosary beads close to her heart, packed the folds of her clothes with packets of herbs. Mother hid extra food inside her apron and I tucked my bow and axe inside my belt before wrapping a large blanket over my shoulders to hide the sharp protruding edges. I would not leave without my bow and axe no matter whose terms came down from on high.

I drew in a long hard breath and held it. My eyes became watery. If Moore wanted me out of the Castillo, he would have to murder me where I stood or carry me out himself.

The watchtower bell suddenly came to life. The sentry stood at the edge of the gun deck. "Governor Moore and his troops approach the gate!"

Juan Felipe and a crew of soldiers cleared the crowd from the entrance.

Governor Zúñiga entered the courtyard; his officers huddled close to his side. The governor looked straight ahead, his tired eyes flittering across the wall of anxious faces as he turned his full attention to the entrance. His surrounding officers stood beside him, showing no signs of fear. Uncle Manuel's injured arm dangled limply at his side as he held his head high and moved stoically toward the front.

"Your uncle does not wear his sling," said Miguel. "The thorns inside his wound must be causing him great pain."

I clenched my hands shut, trying to shake the dreadful feeling consuming my guts. The knot in my throat started to throb. My voice cracked. "Uncle Manuel does not want to appear weak in front of the enemy."

"How so?" whispered Miguel.

"The governor must negotiate from a position of strength, if our surrender is to be taken seriously. We are still in danger. If Moore does not allow the townspeople safe passage out of the territory, we are unable to stop him." I turned and faced Miguel. "Those brave men are sacrificing themselves, Miguel. Uncle Manuel's shoulder is of no concern to him now. Moore does not intend to let Governor Zúñiga or his officers live."

Miguel swallowed but did not speak. My own throat felt as if someone had squeezed the life from it. I struggled to breathe.

Nico trailed some distance behind his father, his face heavy with worry. For the first time in my life, I felt great pity for him. It was his father and my uncle that we watched marching toward death and we could do nothing to save him. My breath came in short gasps.

Governor Zúñiga stopped at the entrance and waited for the

bridge to lower. His eyes, ringed in dark circles, stared straight ahead. Uncle Manuel and the other officers did not show any thought or emotion. It became so quiet that a baby yawning next to us attracted the attention of those around.

Then the piercing banging of the tower bell shattered the quiet. The crowd looked up to see members of the garrison waving their arms frantically in the air from the gun deck. "Governor! Four men-o'-war approach on the horizon!"

The governor turned his head toward the gun deck but did not make any movements. At first, excitement rippled across the crowd, then voices full of fear. "We are saved! *La Gloria* returns!" . . . "No, they are English and they have brought bombs!" . . . "They ready to fire on the Castillo!" . . . "Sign the contract with Moore before he changes his mind!" . . . "Hurry! Save us, Governor!"

Chaos erupted. People began pushing and pulling against each other. The garrison closed ranks to block the path to the gate, but the crowd did not stop advancing. The front of the line was trampled as people pushed from the back. The people closest to the soldiers tried to back away but those behind them were unable to move because of the crowd pushing forward. The garrison lowered their muskets into position with bayonets out.

"LISTEN!" I screamed. "If they are Spanish and we walk into Moore's hands, we will have doomed ourselves before help arrives!"

The crowd continued to push forward.

"They cannot hear you!" yelled Miguel. "This crowd is mad with fear!"

I could not hear the governor give the order, but I saw him signal the men to stop lowering the bridge. The wooden structure froze halfway down, abandoning Moore and his men on the other side of the bridge. Uncle Manuel shouted out orders, clearing a path to the battlements for the governor and officers. Miguel and I followed them up the ramp behind Nico.

Juan Felipe handed the field glass to the governor. Four tiny dots appeared on the horizon, a distance too far away to recognize the allegiance of their flags. The governor studied the position of the ships and the surrounding enemy. No one moved. A biting winter wind rolling off the ocean pounded the gun deck.

I pulled the blanket across my shoulders up over my head and buried my fingers inside. My frozen ears ached from the cold and I could no longer feel my fingers. We shifted back and forth in the freezing wind, waiting.

Uncle Manuel studied the horizon. "The men-o'-war do not move toward the Castillo. Their position remains unchanged."

"Perhaps they are English and wait for orders," said Juan Felipe.

Uncle Manuel shook his head. "That would explain Moore's declaration of strength. He knew of their arrival."

I felt empty inside. Miguel looked down at the ground next to me. I shifted uneasily in place, waiting for the governor to leave his place on the battlements and order the garrison to lower the gate again. I closed my eyes. We, the people of the Castillo, had no choice but to surrender to Moore. We were damned.

The governor moved back to the eastern wall and handed the field glass to Uncle Manuel.

I wrung my hands in worry, desperately trying to recall Grandpapa's words. War is about deception . . . the skillful leader subdues the enemy without fighting . . . avoid what is strong and strike at what is weak.

But the Castillo could do nothing. We were the weaker force. My bottom lip quivered. My heart ached. I'm sorry, Grandpapa, but I do not know what to do.

Closing my eyes, I drew in a deep breath. I was not a seasoned soldier. Only weeks ago, I was but a boy. I grew food in the fields, hunted for herbs in the woods, attended to the animals, traded with the Indians, helped my grandpapa, and hunted. I was a hunter.

Then I opened my eyes. I turned quickly to view the fort as the ships on the horizon would see us. As a hunter, I must think like the prey to understand what the prey will do. When a buck runs, I must understand where it will flee and why. If the sea is on one side and rocky cliffs fill the other, the deer will take the path straight ahead. The prey must choose between danger and safety.

If a rescue ship enters the harbor, it must know what danger lies ahead. It must measure its moves against the forces surrounding it.

I stared at the English ships anchored outside our harbor. If the men-o'-war were English, they would sail amongst friends. They did not risk capture or confrontation, but if the ships were Spanish, it was the enemy who filled the waters. They would not willingly sail into a lion's den.

Envisioning my view from a deck sitting on the horizon, I saw cannons ready on the battlements. Men too small to distinguish walked across the gun deck. An English army stood outside the entrance ready to enter. The fort appeared to have fallen.

Then my eyes fell upon the empty flag pole and my understanding became clear.

"Governor, we must raise our flag! The men-o'-war hesitate because they do not know who occupies the fort!"

***

IT FILLS ME WITH gladness to say things moved rapidly after that and our many, many weeks of prayers were answered. The garrison ran our flag up the pole. The wind unfurled the Spanish red serrated cross in all its majesty like a beacon for the Crown. The Spanish men-o'-war did not engage the enemy but drew closer to the harbor so all could see the color of their flags and the might of their cannons. Eight English prows turned to leave and the exit began.

As it turns out, Moore had not captured the garrison in Apalachee, nor had he received reinforcements. When he and his army realized their deception was no longer possible, they unleashed a wrath of fury by setting fire to the city before leaving. Governor Zúñiga ordered the garrison to fire the cannons, hoping the concussions would dampen the flames, but the ferocious blaze continued to burn until the city became ash.

Despite Moore's destruction, the spirit of the people remained unbroken and the city of St. Augustine was rebuilt. As for Ranson, he returned and Governor Zúñiga awarded the pirate a full pardon for his brave deeds and loyalty to the Spanish Crown. When Miguel and I came of age, we donned our uniforms with pride and gladly took the rank of soldier.

Author's Note

UNDER SIEGE! IS A FICTIONAL ADVENTURE created around the 1702 siege of St. Augustine, Florida. A lot of imagination blended with historical fact brought this story to life. When I first read the historical account of the 1702 siege, I felt as if I were reading the screenplay for a Hollywood movie. Danger, adventure, espionage, and a pirate! I couldn't wait to see what the two fictional characters, Pedro and Miguel, would do. As a teacher by day and a writer during the summer, I spent six years writing this story. It is my hope that readers will not only enjoy the adventure but also feel the hard times, the emotional angst of the colonial era, and the sacrifices that came with building an empire. But most important of all, *Under Siege!* is a tale of an ancient city on its way to becoming the "oldest city" in America.

For easier identification, many of the English names used today, such as Amelia Island instead of Santa Maria Island, have remained the same.

Two books proved invaluable in my writing of this book:

The Art of War by Sun Tzu. 1910 Translation by Lionel Giles, (1875–1978).

The Siege of St. Augustine in 1702 by Charles W. Arnade. St. Augustine Historical Society, University of Florida Press, Gainesville, 1959.

Historical Notes

NO ONE TODAY LIVED at the time of the 1702 siege. If they did, we would have a first-hand account of events. In order to recreate a time from the past, we rely on historians who search for records left behind and archaeologists who unearth artifacts. Dr. Charles W. Arnade of the University of Florida was one of those historians who, in 1958, did extensive research on the 1702 siege. It is the evidence that he uncovered that gave life to this story. As a teacher and writer, I wove the facts outlined in Arnade's monograph into an adventure.

So, you may ask, what part of this story is true? The short answer is, a great deal of it, down to the type of ships anchored out at sea and the instruments they played at the Christmas celebration. The town of St. Augustine, Florida, and the fort called the Castillo de San Marcos are real places. English Governor James Moore of Carolina was a real person. Wanting to diminish the Spanish threat to his territory, he organized an attack against St. Augustine. It was his war. The details of Moore's strength and how the Spanish were ill-prepared are true. Governor Zúñiga, a real person with siege experience, did historically receive word from a Chacato woman of the attack beforehand. From that knowledge, he ordered the inhabitants and the neighboring tribes into the Castillo de San Marcos, ruining the easy victory the English had expected.

It was a fact that Governor Zúñiga would not let boys under the age of fourteen serve. The fictional characters Pedro and Miguel, and their frustration at not being allowed to serve, arose from that fact. The Castillo was built with coquina stone (made from seashells). This produced a surprising result that most probably changed the course of the siege. Walls made of coquina are somewhat soft so cannonballs tend to sink into rather than break them. Enemy trenches were actually dug up to firing range. Enemy spies were real. Ammunition became critically low. Storms were a problem. Slave hunters combed the area. Running out of food was a real concern.

I tried to stay true to the actual facts and timeline as much as possible. Research from resources and experts provided rich content for the era. In places where it was not so clear, imagination and storytelling took precedence. For instance, the pirate Andrew Ranson was a real prisoner at the fort. His history is real as was his release from jail because the soldiers could not attend to the prisoners. It is true the Spanish were concerned about his actions since he was an Englishman. As a storyteller, I created a "what if" scenario. The story of Ranson commandeering a brigantine out from under the enemy's nose was storytelling and not a recorded event. But it was true that the Spanish feared the enemy would bring a sixteen-pound cannon and mortar to breach the Castillo's walls. It is also true that the governor later pardoned the pirate.

You can visit St. Augustine, Florida, and feel history come alive in this oldest European-settled town in the continental United States. The Castillo de San Marcos still stands there on Matanzas Bay as a national park. When you stand in the courtyard, you will remember the people held there in the siege of 1702. And when you stand on the ramparts you can imagine the British ships out in the bay, their guns facing you.

Glossary

Apalachee: northwestern Florida

bandolier: a broad belt having a number of small loops for holding chargers of gunshot, worn over the shoulder by soldiers

bastion: a projecting part of a wall, rampart, or other fortification. The diamond shaped structures of the Castillo de San Marcos are bastions.

battery: a unit of cannons (guns) together with the artillerymen and the equipment required to operate them

bayonet: a long knife fixed at the end of a flintlock and used as a weapon

blacksmith: someone who forges and shapes iron with a hammer and anvil

blunderbuss: a short musket of wide bore with a flared muzzle

bombardment: heavy fire of artillery

booty: goods or money obtained illegally

bounty: reward, payment

brigantine: a two-masted sailing ship that is square-rigged except for a fore-and-aft mainsail

budge barrel: a small copper-hooped barrel with only one head, the other end being closed by a piece of leather, which is drawn together with strings like a purse. It is used for carrying powder from the magazine to the battery.

cannon: a large artillery gun usually on wheels that uses gunpowder to launch projectiles

charger: individual wooden bottle (flask) of gun powder charges, attached to a bandolier

cocoplum: small, white or purplish thin skinned fleshy fruits

coquina: a porous stone mixture made from ancient layers of shells (coquina clams) found in the southern United States

criollos: locally born descendants of European Spanish

cutlass: a short, heavy sword with a curved blade that was commonly used by sailors and pirates

cypress knees: knobby root projections that grow above the low-lying water around a cypress tree

dandy: a man who is overly concerned about fashionable clothing and has mannerisms like those in the aristocracy

field glass: telescope, spyglass

flag/banner bearer: young boy who carries the country's flag into battle

flintlock: a heavy, long gun that uses sparks from striking flint to ignite the gunpowder inside the pan

friar: a member of a religious group in Catholic Christianity

friary: a monastery (residence) of friars, a house for persons under religious vows

frigate: medium-size square-rigged warship

gabion: a basket or cage filled with earth or rocks and used above the ground to line trenches so the enemy cannot shoot into the trenches

garita: an overhanging, wall-mounted turret projecting from the walls of a fort used for look-out

garrison: the military soldiers who guard a fortification

garrote: An instrument for execution by strangulation

glacis: the sloping ground built up around the outside of a fort that helps protect the walls from enemy fire

Gobernador y *Capitán General*: governor and high-ranking general captain

gopher tortoise: burrowing land tortoise of southeastern North America

gundeck: deck holding cannons

hardtack: a nonperishable hard cracker made of water and flour kept for nourishment during long periods without food

Havana: capital of Cuba

knucklebones: game of jacks played in various ways with knuckles from a sheep

linstock: a staff about a meter long with a point on one end for sticking into the ground. It holds a smoldering rope tip used for igniting.

longboat: a large boat launched by a sailing vessel for transportation

magnolia: large flower-producing tree with large broad leaves

maize: corn

man-o'-war: a ship with many weapons (cannons) used for war

matchcord: a cord carried loosely in the hand or hooked to the belt. It was lighted at one or both ends when carried into action.

mestizo: a person of mixed European and Native American ancestry

mortar: a very short cannon aimed upward for lobbing shells at an arched angle

mullato: a person with mixed white and black ancestry

munitions: collection of weapons

muscadine grapes: grapes with a tough skin native to the American South

musket: a heavy-muzzle front-loading long gun used before the invention of the rifle

musketeers: foot soldiers armed with muskets

Native Indians: local Native Americans originating from the area *niño*: Spanish for boy

Nombre de Dios mission: a Christian church started in 1565 when Menéndez founded St. Augustine. It is now recognized as the first permanent Christian church in the U.S. The mission offered religious education to Native tribes.

palisade: a fence made of stakes driven into the ground for protection

palmetto: spiny-toothed palm plant with fan-like leaves

pantalones: Spanish for trousers

patriot: one who loves and fights for his or her country

patron saint: a saint who defends a group or nation

Pensacola: a town in far northeast Florida

persimmon: an orange, plum-like fruit

pond apple: fruit of a small evergreen tree

portcullis: gate consisting of an iron or wooden grating that hangs in the entry to a castle or fortified town; can be lowered to prevent passage

port sally: a secure entryway of a series of doors or gates

privateers: crewmembers of a ship commissioned to rob merchants' ships

repast: meal, food served and eaten at one time

palisade: fortification consisting of a strong fence made of stakes driven into the ground

port: left side of a ship to a person facing the bow

poultice: a medical treatment (dressing) that is spread on a cloth and applied to the skin to treat wounds

quarter-pike: a small heavy spear with a wooden shaft, one-quarter the size of a regular eighteen- to twenty-foot pike used by the infantry (thus four to five feet long)

sally: to set out in a sudden, energetic action

salt fish: fish dried and preserved with salt

sandbar: an area in the water where ocean waves deposit sand into a barrier

sawgrass: a plant distinguished by tiny, sharp spines covering the surface of its leaves

sloop: a small warship with guns (cannons) on only one deck

spiritualist: someone who senses the presence of spirits

St. Johns River: a river in northeast Florida, modern name of Rio de San Mateo, and its later name, Rio de San Juan

stern: the rear part of a ship

swamp cabbage: heart of the cabbage palm, used for food

Timucua: indigenous people of northeast and north central Florida, now extinct

treasure fleet: a convoy of ships traveling back and forth from Spain to the New World transporting goods and treasure

trench: a deep, long, narrow ditch dug into the ground used as protection for soldiers

vihuelas: a guitar-shaped instrument with six sets of double strings

winch: a lifting device used on a ship to lift heavy objects from and to the cargo hold

Yamasee Indians: indigenous native tribe of the Georgia and northeast Florida coast, allied with the English

yaupon holly: a plant used by Native Americans to make a tea and the black drink used in rituals

Acknowledgments

THIS BOOK would not have been possible without the help of so many passionate people. I am grateful to everyone who was involved in the writing of this book. Dr. Arnade's detailed monograph on the Siege of 1702 provided a rich historical account of the event. Joseph Brehm, of the Castillo de San Marcos, generously shared his bountiful knowledge of the fort. Reader, teacher, and historian Jake Harper broke out the books, dusted off his research notes, and brought the story to task. My heartfelt thanks to Kelley Weitzel MacCabe for her willingness to share her extensive knowledge of the indigenous Timucua people, and last but not least, a special thank you to my husband, Gary, for his undying love of the story and his watchful eye over the boys, Pedro and Miguel.

Here are some other books from Pineapple Press on related topics. For a complete catalog, visit our website at pineapplepress.com. Or write to Pineapple Press, P.O. Box 3889, Sarasota, Florida 34230-3889, or call (800) 746-3275.

America's REAL First Thanksgiving by Robyn Gioia. When most Americans think of the first Thanksgiving, they think of the Pilgrims and the Indians in New England in 1621. But on September 8, 1565, the Spanish and the native Timucua celebrated with a feast of Thanksgiving in St. Augustine. Teacher's activity guide also available. Ages 9–14.

Escape to the Everglades by Edwina Raffa and Annelle Rigsby. Based on historical fact, this young adult novel tells the story of Will Cypress, a half-Seminole boy living among his mother's people during the Second Seminole War. He meets Chief Osceola and travels with him to St. Augustine. Ages 9–14.

A Land Remembered, Student Edition by Patrick Smith. The sweeping story of three generations of MacIveys, who work their way up from a dirt-poor Cracker life to the wealth and standing of real estate tycoons. Volume 1 covers the first generation of MacIveys to arrive in Florida and Zech's coming of age. Volume 2 covers Zech's son, Solomon, and the exploitation of the land as his own generation prospers. Ages 9 and up.

Solomon by Marilyn Bishop Shaw. Eleven-year-old Solomon Freeman and his parents survive the Civil War, gain their freedom, and gamble their dreams, risking their very existence on a homestead in the remote environs of north central Florida. Ages 9–14.

The Spy Who Came In from the Sea by Peggy Nolan. In 1943 fourteen-year-old Frank Holleran sees an enemy spy land on Jacksonville Beach. First Frank needs to get people to believe him, and then he needs to stop the spy from carrying out his dangerous plans. Winner of the Sunshine State Young Reader's Award. Ages 8–12.